THE GOLD DEADLINE

THE GOLD DEADLINE

A WHODUNIT

Herbert Resnicow

A
Joan
Kahn
BOOK

St. Martin's Press
New York

Library of Congress Cataloging in Publication Data

Resnicow, Herbert.
   The gold deadline.

   "A Joan Kahn book."
   I. Title.
PS3568.E69G58   1984   813'.54   83-26953
ISBN 0-312-33162-2

First Edition
10 9 8 7 6 5 4 3 2 1

To my beloved wife, Melly

The names of real people and organizations of the ballet world are occasionally mentioned in this book. If my respect, admiration and love of these great artists and companies is not sufficiently evident, it is due only to lack of literary skills.

The first ballet I saw was "Les Sylphides." I was seventeen.

Herbert Resnicow

For once, it wasn't entirely my husband's fault. Not that Alexander was completely innocent—that's something he never was and never will be, not while I'm around—but the brunt of the blame must fall on the narrow padded shoulders of Burton Hanslik, world's richest mouthpiece and rotten husband—grade two, tops—to my best friend and next-door neighbor, Pearl.

Actually, if you believe in sociologists, Burton was not guilty by reason of environment, having been married to Pearl for twenty-five years. A layman might expect that, after such long experience, a husband would realize that his wife thought with her glands, but when those glands measure thirty-four D in front of a ninety-eight-pound, five-foot-short body garnished with heavy golden hair down to its *tochus*—in men, for some well-known reason, there is a sudden shortage of blood to the higher thought centers. Even my husband, who is as much smarter than Burton as Burton is than the average lawyer, melts when Pearl turns on her big brown eyes. In fact there were times when she had conned me into doing something I positively knew was moronic and I actually knowingly did it, and I'm a woman, so I really feel for the poor, helpless, filthy little beasts.

Alexander and I were sitting in the first floor living room of our brownstone with the door closed because we were watching "Rumpole of the Bailey" on public television. Not that there's anyone else in the house to disturb us, but my husband requires a special ritual for Horace Rumpole: the door closed, curtains and drapes drawn (although there is very little traffic on West 74th Street), iced cocoa handy (in case his brain should dim from lack of sustenance), black leather recliner—the one I bought when I finally learned he would be released from the intensive coronary care unit—tilted back at exactly the right angle, and the lights low, to focus the experience sharply.

Alexander loves that show because Horace Rumple is such a character. Horace Rumple would adore Alexander Magnus Gold for exactly the same reason, in spades. Doubled. Make that redoubled.

I am not allowed to talk as we watch the fat, sloppy, wily old barrister twist British law to his own mischievous ends. Not that Alexander can't do two things at once, or three or four—I've often carried on a conversation with him while he played chess, read a book, and watched TV, God forbid he should give me his full attention—but he wants to concentrate all parts of his coordinated mind on that extraordinary production, down to the location of cigar ashes on Rumpole's vest, and point these all out to me, although this is the third time we've watched the show. But, to be truthful, each time we watched, Alexander discovered some new subtle delight that we had not noticed before.

Near the show's end there was a knock on the living-room door. It had to be Pearl, who else? She and I had exchanged keys years ago, making it easier to get deliveries from Bloomingdale's, to take care of each other in sickness, and to have our daily coffee and gossip in the afternoon. Burton has a key too, but he would just walk in. Pearl acts as if there were all sorts of sexy romantic goings-on behind my closed living-room door. Fat chance. After twenty-seven years of mar-riage—I was a child bride, eighteen, but big for my age— husbands do not rip off filmy negligees in the living room, not off their own wives, at least, as Pearl must know having just celebrated her silver, because Bloomingdale's charges much more for black satin with holes in it than without, and if a wife gets to like the sound of ripping lingerie, a husband could go broke very rapidly.

The trouble with Pearl is that she's read so many sexy French novels—her doctorate is in comparative literature —that she's come to believe that real life is like feelthy peectures. Or could her knock mean that she's trying to make me subtly believe that she and Burton . . . ? Nah, Pearl wouldn't dare try that on me.

When he heard the knock, Alexander, without taking his eyes off the TV, barked, "Norma," and pointed to the door. It wasn't his congenital impoliteness that bothered me; I'm a big girl and I can open doors by myself. It was his implicit, which he would gladly have explicited, assumption that, in watching "Rumpole," the one who understood and ap-preciated the finer points better (husband) should not have to take his eyes off the tube as long as there was in the room a duller entity (wife) for whom missing seven details would not constitute so great a loss.

Pearl, guaranteed, was waiting politely for us to adjust our passionate deshabille so, to make her happy, I misbut-toned my blouse before I opened the door—the things I do to let the poor innocent keep her illusions.

Burton walked in smelling like a barber shop. As I bent down to kiss him—he's only two inches taller than Alex-ander—I wondered what childish romantic plot Pearl had cooked up this time that warranted Burton's shaving at ten o'clock on a Sunday night just to visit his closest friends next door. Wearing a jacket and tie, yet.

Pearl, in worn jeans and a loose sweater, looked like an undernourished overdeveloped teenybopper: no makeup, skin like cream, hair down to here. Out of respect for her age—she's one year older—I didn't kill her, only prayed she should get a pimple, just once in her life, for not calling that she was bringing Burton all dressed up. It's not that I'm vain, but at my height a little fresh lipstick never hurts.

Knowing Alexander, they sat down to wait quietly. When "Rumpole" was over Alexander switched off the TV and said, "I hope you realize what a sacrifice I'm making, Burton; I wouldn't miss "Fawlty Towers" for anyone but you. If you wanted to drop over, why not this afternoon?"

"Couldn't," Burton answered in his pear-shaped barrister's voice. "We just came from Max Baron's house."

"He needs a criminal lawyer? On a Sunday? I thought billionaires just whispered 'Kill! Kill!' and three vice-presidents got the victim's blood all over their gray flannels."

"My firm also has a very fine corporate division, Alec, which handles much of Baron's out-of-house work. And Pearl and I are very close to the Barons socially. I'm attorney for the Foundation, I sit on several boards with Max, and we're on the executive committee of some fund-raising organizations. Pearl is practically a protégée of Julia Baron's; she's grooming Pearl for some big jobs in her favorite charities." Now I knew why Pearl had put on sloppies; she didn't want to sit next to me dressed the way she had to be with a billionaire's wife.

"The answer is no." Alexander stood up to his full five foot six. "Positively no." He really looked good at two hundred fifteen, having dropped twenty-five pounds under my watchful eye since his heart attack. His waist was slim, relatively, his huge arm muscles well defined—not like a bodybuilder's, naturally, powerlifters tend to look like barrels rather than Adonises—but compared to what he used to be? Beautiful. And he hadn't used a nitroglycerine pill for angina for over two weeks now. If I could get him down below two hundred, I could feel safe. "I don't want a job, even with Max Baron."

"What are you talking about, Alec?" Burton asked. "Who mentioned a job?"

"It's obvious. A lawyer spending an evening with a big industrialist client—what do you talk about? Sex?"

"Come on, Alec, the man is sixty-five. Of course we talked business. But we discussed other things too."

"Granted." Alexander sat down. "But then you come right here. Sunday night. And you shaved first to look your persuasive best. So confess. One of his companies is in trouble. You tell him you have a friend, an engineer, who is a genius, aggressive, a generalist who can learn anything in two weeks. He tells you to get this guy, quietly, discreetly, not through the normal channels, make him president suddenly on Monday morning, clean sweep, get rid of the deadwood, turn the company around, put the fear of God into the other companies, right?"

"Wrong." Burton looked amused. "But close."

"Well, I won't do it." Alexander scowled. "I've been my own boss for twenty years now, and I'll never be an employee again, at any level. I've made enough money from the Talbott case to last for quite a while, so tell Max Baron if he wants a consultant, I'll talk business. Otherwise, no."

"Good," said Burton. "Subject to one minor condition, I am authorized to retain you as a consultant to solve a problem Baron has. Name your fee, Alec."

"No fees, Burton; you know how I work. The client has a problem. When I solve it, I get a big reward. If I fail, I get nothing. And I eat all the expenses."

"How does one hundred thousand sound, Alec?"

"Depends on the problem. Talk."

Burton leaned forward and spoke in a whisper. "A billionaire does not work, in the usual sense, although he is at work every moment of his waking hours. He receives information, integrates it, makes decisions, and has his executives carry them out. If his decisions are right his industries flourish; his employees eat; his suppliers, his stockholders, the whole economy benefits. If he makes wrong decisions, his empire is wrecked, his employees lose their jobs, stockholders lose their money, the whole country is hurt."

"Don't belabor the obvious." Alexander sounded impatient. "Get to the point."

"These decisions," Burton continued, "whether to expand or contract, buy or sell, borrow or spend, are often made years in advance of the market and cannot be changed easily or economically. It is important that they be kept secret, kept from competitors here and overseas, kept from politicians and government agencies, even from his top executives. This the entrepreneur accomplishes by not telling anyone of his overall plans; by ordering one company to produce one part of the design, another to do another part, but never revealing enough for anyone to see the pattern."

"Sounds reasonable," Alexander said. "What's Baron's problem?"

"Someone's reading his mind."

"Are you serious, Burton?"

"Baron is. He senses that the market knows what his decisions are, although they are not in writing or recorded in any way."

"Senses?" Alexander, the engineer, thinks he makes only rational decisions based solely on data. Hah!

"Business, at Baron's level, is tremendously complex," Burton explained. "Literally an infinity of connections and relations. There is no way anyone, using all the computers in the world, could record, much less correlate, even one minute's worth of all the variables that affect an economy. Even if you could, how would you weight them? How would your own efforts invalidate your information? And the minutes keep running on and on, in real time. Baron must work in real time; he senses trends, patterns, and then makes his plans, decisions, corrections, whatever has to be done. It's almost unconscious."

"A pattern maker?" Alexander perked up.

"The best," Burton said decisively.

"Well, now . . ." Alexander tried to look modest, but the flush spread over the top of his head.

"The best," Burton repeated. "You're good, Alec, probably the best of your type, but you work with facts; you analyze, put pieces together, think. Max Baron just knows."

"If he's that good, why doesn't he solve his own problem?"

"He tried; got nowhere. Probably because he's too close to the situation. Like trying to operate on your own brain. Pearl suggested that maybe a rational analytical approach would help. She recommended you."

"No," Alexander said. "It can't be done. Impossible. For me to have any chance at all, I'd have to know the one thing he can't tell anyone: his plans."

"He knows that; that's the minor condition I mentioned before. He wants to meet you first. Then if he decides to retain you, he'll tell you everything, which he can't do with an outside agency or even his own security people."

It had to be Pearl. I gave her a look. She nodded and said, "I told Julia Baron that Alex was trustworthy." Just like that. Simple. I get funny looks even when I pay in cash, but Pearl just smiles and billionaires risk their empires on her judgment.

"I take it he's too busy to come to my office," Alexander

said. "Where is his office and what time tomorrow morning should I be there?"

"He has a set of offices in midtown," Burton said, "but he's rarely there. When he's not visiting his companies, he works out of his apartment."

"A billionaire lives in an apartment house?" I couldn't believe this.

"Not quite," Burton answered me. "He has one floor of a small brownstone on the East Side, which he rents monthly. The servants and security people live on the other floors. He and Julia live very simply."

"Why doesn't he buy the building?" I asked.

"I'll explain everything later," Pearl said. "We came here tonight to make sure you have Thursday night open. We're all going to the Gala Farewell Performance of the Boguslav Ballet Russe as guests of the Barons."

"How do you hold a business meeting at the ballet?" I asked. "And why the Boguslav?" Pearl was studiously looking too innocent. Definitely something fishy going on, but I didn't see what. Yet.

"Baron's Foundation is a big contributor to the Boguslav," Burton answered, "and Baron's son, Jeffrey, is Viktor Boguslav's personal assistant. It's a good cover, Alec, meeting socially; after all, you have had your picture in the papers as a detective, and Baron doesn't want to be seen consulting you professionally."

"You'll like Julia Baron, Norma," Pearl said, too cheerfully. "She's not that much older than we are and I told her all about you." Fishier and fishier Pearl. "And you'll just love her daughters; Susan is a living doll and Roberta is just like you, Norma, very bright, I mean."

"So there'll be nine of us for the evening?" I asked.

"Jeffrey has to stay with Viktor Boguslav," Burton said. "There will be eight of us in the box."

"So when do I talk to Max Baron?" Alexander asked.

"The Boguslav is leaving for a Russian tour next Sunday night, and Max Baron is giving a big farewell dinner on Thursday for the whole company after the Gala Benefit Performance."

"That's when Mr. Baron will decide if he wants to retain me?" Alexander asked. "That's when we talk?"

"Exactly," Burton replied, "so be on your best behavior. Especially you, Norma. No wisecracks about grinding widows and orphans."

I smiled sweetly. "Does that mean that you and Pearl have to be especially super-nice to me for the next four days, otherwise I fix it so you lose your biggest client?"

Burton paled, but Pearl looked happy. "Then you'll come?" she asked.

Alexander looked the question at me; I nodded. What could we lose? No one would be shooting at me, like in the Talbott case. We certainly could use the money, in spite of how rich my husband thought we were, and I have a strong need to tell a live billionaire what I think of live billionaires.

I stood up to my full six foot one and placed one hand on Burton's head and the other on Pearl's. "I've always wanted to have a pair of mated slaves," I told them. "Now back out of the room, bowing deferentially as you go, to She-Who-Must-Be-Obeyed."

Pearl was delighted. Burton frowned. Alexander looked worried. Funny—he laughs when Rumpole says it.

2

Someday I'm going to kill Pearl. Not right now, in the limousine Max Baron sent to pick us up. Too many witnesses: the chauffeur, who'd have to clean the blood off the upholstery; Alexander who, ignorant of Pearl's perfidy, would try to stop me; Burton who, if he knew how Pearl had used him, would try to stop Alexander from stopping me, although Alexander could tear him apart with one pinky; Susan Baron, the living doll, who probably took after her mother, Pearl's rotten accomplice; and Roberta Baron, the innocent focus of Pearl's melodramatic little cabal.

I'd have to get Pearl alone. Maybe when we got to the theater I'd invite her to go to the powder room with me. She wouldn't dare refuse, which is one of the advantages a person who is a little above average in height has over a skinny blond shrimp, especially since I have a tendency to be slightly a few pounds over, here and there.

"You'll just love her daughters," Pearl had said. Well, I didn't love pretty black-eyed Susan, who clearly had no interest in anyone whose blood was not ninety-proof testosterone, especially if that anyone was old enough to be her mother.

Roberta was really nice, poor girl, with just a few minor

problems. Nothing unusual, the same problems any girl in New York has who is twenty-nine going on thirty-one: finding a single, masculine presentable man who makes a living, eats with a fork, and doesn't turn green if someone hints at marriage.

Roberta's problem was compounded a bit by her being educated—Dr. Roberta Baron, Pearl introduced her—a researcher into synthesizing chlorophyll, and intelligent, as I discovered in our first few minutes of rapidly-escalating-to-higher-level-abstraction conversation, both tremendous obstacles in the reproductive race—for a girl, at least. Dumdum blondes can get away with eyelash-batting and you're-so-wonderfulling when the white knight uses a two-syllable word, but give the filthy little beasts a chance to score with a really super woman and watch them shrink from the opportunity. Worse, Roberta had a sense of humor—limiting her, among New York's teeming millions of the opposition sex, to those two—maybe three, tops—who have cast-iron egos, like my Alexander who, to this day, doesn't realize that he is seven inches shorter than I am.

Roberta was also, obviously, a great reader, as her thick glasses showed. I'd have to take her in hand and explain the facts of contact lenses to her. She was a beautiful girl with long auburn hair drawn tightly back in a bun; not pretty, but beautiful, if you looked carefully; somewhat *zoftig,* but the right man would find her highly edible. I could show her how, with a few minor touches, she could come out of hiding. If she wanted to. Clearly, she didn't. I wondered who had been so cruel to her; why was obvious.

When Pearl said Roberta was just like me, she wasn't lying. As a matter of fact, Pearl's whole amateurish plot, the fantasy of someone's reading Baron's mind, became clear the moment I met Roberta Baron. Roberta, wearing flats, stood one inch taller than I did in low heels. That's it, the whole big deal. If that little blond blonde had come to me openly, would I have refused? Did she think I wouldn't see right through her childish little scenario; that I would let this insult to my intelligence pass unavenged? Let her shrink in the seat behind the shield of Alexander; when we got to the theater I would get her.

One of the reasons I wouldn't mind being a billionaire is that you can get to the theater early, when the lobby is practically empty. "Excuse me," I explained to the others as I took Pearl by the left deltoid and started walking toward the powder room. She tried to make herself heavy, but for someone who has, on occasion, pinned one of the strongest men in New York, a ninety-eight-pound blond weakling is no problem.

I backed her against a stall and stood close to her so she would have to look up at me. "Well?" I said, very politely.

Pearl didn't even have the decency to look up. "She's a nice girl," she muttered in her beard.

"So?" I encouraged.

"Her mother wants her to get married."

"And . . .?"

"I thought that . . ."

"You thought?" I exploded. "You never thought in your life, you walking mammary gland. You felt, you moron, not thought. If I decorticated you right now, no one would notice. Ever. You wanted to show that girl that even a giant klutz like me could get herself a husband, didn't you? If the freak can get a man, anyone can, right? Couldn't you have asked me? Don't I have feelings? Don't I know how people look at me?" I was crying. "Why, Pearl? Why?"

She looked up at me, crying too. "No, Norma, not that. I wanted her to see how wonderful a woman could be, that size doesn't matter, woman or man. That a man as great as Alexander loves you; that a man like that offered to die for you."

"You think it's so easy married to an ego like that, Pearl?
You think it's all fun? Always excitement, tension, no
peace? Worrying if I say the wrong word, will he explode?
Get another heart attack? Die? You think it's so great living
on a peak? You want to try it?"

"You think it's so great, Norma, to live on a plain? Always? Never a peak? Never? Some people would give anything to have just once what you have always. Some people."

I looked into her eyes and saw, for the first time saw,
Pearl, real, my Pearl, deep, her pain, her need, her life, her
love, and together we put our arms around each other and
held each other like women like love like a mother holds her
daughter we were both it's good to have Pearl I need Pearl
I love Pearl.

Makeup repaired, we joined the others in the lobby. Max
and Julia Baron were there. He was tall, very thin, hard,
with stiff straight white hair. His face was sharp, lined, the
high-bridged nose like an ax blade. Julia Baron looked surprisingly young, her soft red hair showing only a few
strands of gray, dressed in a simple long-sleeved high-
necked black gown that nicely showed her slightly plump
figure. The Barons stood together, hands lightly touching,
as we were introduced by Burton.

"I have been looking forward to meeting you, Mr. Gold,
Mrs. Gold," Baron said, a trace of *mittel-Europa* in his voice.
"May I present my wife, Julia?"

Mrs. Baron held Alexander's hand a little longer than the
normal rhythm of the movement required, staring at him
the while, then turned to me and took my right hand in both
of hers. "You are as beautiful," she said very softly, looking
directly into my eyes, "as Pearl told me. I think we will
know each other more." Goddamn Pearl, why hadn't she
ever told me that? Maybe . . . had I ever told Pearl she was

a raving beauty? Even once? Women just don't. We have to get our compliments from men. And then be not sure. Why?

"It's early, but I'd like to go to our box now," Baron said as he shepherded us up the stairs. "It may be possible to see Jeffrey before the performance starts."

The Temple Theater is an anachronism, ornate and plush, overdecorated in what was the height of luxury at the turn of the century, designed for the titled of Europe and the American nobility of money. There is a shallow U of boxes at the Grand Tier level, each of which has a private door, latchable from the inside. The rear of the box is a small cloakroom separated from the seating area in front by a pair of heavy curtains drawn between the short partitions to block anyone in the theater, or even the seats of the box, from looking into the cloak area. As we entered the next-to-the last box on the left side of the theater, Pearl pulled my sleeve. "Isn't this romantic?" she whispered, clearly visualizing the aristocratic liaisons behind the curtain, mirroring the romance simultaneously played out on stage, both to the same rhythm, to the same lovely music, the symbolic affair performed with grace, charm, and beauty, the real one probably poorly cast, badly directed, and consummated without grace.

The Temple had been designed as an opera house, similar to the old Metropolitan, high and shallow, with the perfect acoustics the new opera houses have yet to equal. It was a huge house, with a stage so large that the top curtain was dropped and the side curtains not opened fully.

The Grand Tier boxes swept around the theater without a single column, the bottom of the structure about fifteen feet above the stage level. The front of the end boxes reached about three feet short of the footlights; the rear of the boxes were in line with the proscenium arch.

Over the center of the Grand Tier the First Balcony

stretched across the back of the theater in a shallow arch from wall to wall, also free of columns. There was a shallow Second Balcony near the top of the auditorium, cantilevered out from the back wall. Every seat had a clear view of the stage. For all its age and musty smell, the Temple had a charm, a beauty, and a consideration of its patrons that the modern houses lack. If today's architects can't do better, I thought, they should be honest enough to copy. For what the acoustical changes alone cost at Avery Fisher Hall, we could have had another theater.

We met with a problem: A heavy curtain had been installed between our box and the one on our left, effectively cutting off the view of much of the stage. Max Baron stiffened. "Boguslav did this," he said, and moved toward the curtain. His wife stopped him and quickly said, "Roberta, get Jeffrey."

Roberta was back in a few seconds with a tall harried-looking young man, boyishly handsome, with long red hair. His father silently pointed to the curtain. "It's just this once, Dad," Jeffrey said. "He has to make notes on the performance and doesn't want to disturb anyone."

"I am disturbed more," Baron said, "by the inconvenience of our guests. Please have the curtain removed."

"Please, Dad." Jeffrey looked left to see if Boguslav had heard, and whispered, "You know how he gets. I'll find you another box."

"There is no other box, Jeffrey. I made sure that the house would be full for the Gala Benefit."

"Please, Dad." Jeffrey was almost in tears. "Please." Max Baron glanced at his wife; she put her hand lightly on his arm. Immediately Baron's posture changed. "Go back to the impresario, Jeffrey," he said and turned to us. "We will sit in the best possible way under the circumstances. I in the left front seat with Roberta behind me. Julia, you will sit next to me, Susan behind. Pearl, third front seat, Burton behind; Mr. Gold, fourth front, Mrs. Gold behind." Alexander offered to sit next to the curtain, but Baron overruled him, "This way, considering our respective heights and the angles, we will maximize visibility for us all and my guests will enjoy the ballet. If you were host, Mr. Gold, you would do the same. Please."

I was looking forward to this performance. At least two of the ballets would be good, especially the show-closer, and usually the show-stopper, Tudor's comic virtuoso piece, *Gala Performance,* the funny, boisterous behind-the-scenes story of three competing prima ballerinas. Dancing in it were, indeed, three competing prima ballerinas: Tatiana Kusnitzova of the Boguslav, Irina Trebshinska of Ballet Theater, donating her services for the Benefit, and Tamara Boruskaya, newly defected from the Kirov, making her first American appearance. In the ballet, as in real life, the competition gets a bit rough. People who think ballet companies are full of dainty little angels have fairies at the bottom of their garden. Nobody gets to the top in any field by being a violet, and those ethereal little girls who float wispily across the stage go through a regimen every day that would kill a linebacker.

The middle ballet was *Petrouchka,* my favorite: the bittersweet story of Petrouchka, the doll with the sad clown face, who had a soul, who comes to life for a short time, yearns for freedom, falls in love, and is killed for his humanity.

It takes place at the Shrovetide fair in St. Petersburg. The Charlatan, who owns the Puppet Theater, exhibits his three puppets: the coarse, lustful Moor, the beautiful delicate Ballerina, and Petrouchka, his soul trapped behind a clown face, his heart hidden in a rag-doll body. The Charlatan sounds his flute and the three dolls come to life and dance.

The Moor and Petrouchka contest for the Ballerina, who favors the Moor. Jealously, Petrouchka attacks his rival whereupon the Charlatan stops the play and the dolls stiffen into immobility again.

The Charlatan throws the limp Petrouchka into his bare cell. Petrouchka tries to escape, but it is hopeless; he is doomed, able to come to life only when the Charlatan permits. Petrouchka dances a clumsy stiff-armed imitation of human passion; it is clear that inside his sawdust-stuffed body he feels, hopes, loves.

The Ballerina comes into Petrouchka's cell. In his rapture, he leaps clumsily and violently, frightening the Ballerina, who flees. Despairing of his fate, puppet to the Charlatan, a clown to his beloved Ballerina, mute and stiff, Petrouchka throws himself around the cell and crashes a hole in its wall.

The Moor, meanwhile, is lounging animal-like in his luxurious room. The Ballerina enters and is entranced by the exotic Moor. He drags her to his couch and starts to make love to her. Petrouchka breaks in and, misunderstanding, tries to save the Ballerina from the Moor. He attacks wildly, but the Moor draws his scimitar and tries to kill Petrouchka. The little clown escapes and runs away.

Outside the Puppet Theater, the crowd at the Fair dances wildly, unaware of the drama played out behind the curtains of the Theater. Suddenly Petrouchka comes running out, chased by the Moor. The Moor corners Petrouchka, raises his scimitar, and kills the helpless, trembling little clown. A policeman brings out the Charlatan. The puppetmaster picks up the limp rag-doll and shows the policeman that Petrouchka is made of rags and sawdust, and could never have lived.

The crowd leaves, and the Charlatan, alone in the dark, drags the limp puppet into the Theater. There is a crash of

Petrouchka's theme music. The Charlatan looks up. On top of the Puppet Theater the unconquerable spirit of Petrouchka, the real Petrouchka, defiant, shakes his fist at the Charlatan, as the ballet ends.

This was to be the farewell performance of the legendary Pierre Romanoff, around whom Viktor Boguslav had formed the Boguslav Ballet Russe twenty years ago. Betsy Gilman, the tiny, brilliant, undisciplined young star, who had been in every ballet company in America, would dance the Ballerina, and Kurt Tindall, he of the great *élévation,* would play the Moor.

Viktor Boguslav would not be the Charlatan tonight, which was a pity. His huge bulk made the tiny dancers truly look like puppets, and he acted the part with flair, snapping his whip as though he really was the Charlatan. It was well known that Boguslav was a frustrated dancer, as aren't we all, and never missed an opportunity to appear on stage. There are very few roles in ballet for nondancers, and most of these involve standing around and looking like a king. For Boguslav to miss this one, the best of them all, was strange.

The first ballet on the program was the one that troubled me. One of the reasons I loved the Boguslav, which is nowhere near as perfect as the City Ballet or as versatile as Ballet Theater or as daring as the Nederlands, was that it played the old songs, mine and Alexander's. Where else could we see *Judgment of Paris, Three Virgins and a Devil, Spectre of the Rose, Bluebeard,* and especially, *Les Sylphides,* that deceptively simple, sweet, lovely, romantic set of dances that no one else seemed to be able to do properly today? The Boguslav was as great an anachronism as the Temple Theater, and I loved them both.

But Viktor Boguslav had chosen, amazingly, to present at a farewell gala, a world premiere, *Graven Image,* by that wild man of choreography, Charles Augustine. Boguslav, who had never before even used a ballet less than twenty years old, had commissioned, and paid for, a new, modern, guaranteed unorthodox, probably lousy, ballet.

Even more surprising, instead of using music in the public domain, an original score had also been commissioned by Boguslav from, of all people, Desmond Juspada, who sneered at twelve-tone music as being too melodic. Juspada would also conduct tonight, which, I am sure, made Evan Spenser, the music director, very happy.

Viktor Boguslav was definitely an eccentric, to understate it, in a field noted for eccentrics, in dress, in manner, in physique, in everything, but no one had ever accused him of being crazy, or of spending money unnecessarily (he was, after all, an impresario), or of not loving ballet. But there was no explanation in the program of what he had in mind, nothing in the papers, and even Pearl's friends in the ballet world, where *nothing* is secret, could only guess in frustration at his motive in presenting *Graven Image*.

At least there was one thing in *Graven Image* that both Alexander and I could enjoy: Danilo Hurkos, the undefeated Mr. Galaxy for seven straight years, was in the role, certainly nondancing, of the Ba'aal. Even Alexander didn't know what that was. "Doesn't look like a typo," he said. "Maybe a corruption of Baal." The program gave no hint; instead of a summary of the ballet it simply said, "A work of art stands on its own." Anyway, I love to look at well-built men in tights, or less, and if Hurkos grew a beard, he could pass for the Farnese Hercules. Alexander doesn't care much for body-builders, but he respected Hurkos because he was tremendously strong as well as perfectly proportioned.

I saw Max Baron place his hand on his wife's and, inspired, I bent forward and kissed Alexander on his bald head. He leaned back, enjoying the contact and the love, and reached his hand back to clasp mine for a while.

Well, two good ballets and one that would be, at least, an interesting experience. I moved so I could see between Pearl and Alexander, and prepared to enjoy the fireworks.

3

I could hear the curtains open. The stage was in total darkness, not even the usual little technical lights from the wings. Suddenly there was a great flash directed at the audience and a great bang of sound, a single pluck of the same note on every stringed instrument in the orchestra, echoed immediately by all the percussion three tones lower. Then silence.

As my vision cleared, I could make out the clump of dancers, naked under formless gray gauze, on the bare center stage against a dull black backdrop, slowly expanding outward in all directions. The Big Bang Theory comes to ballet, obviously. When the dancers filled the stage they stopped, waiting, aimless, amorphous. Almost inaudibly, a single thin low sustained violin tone, without vibrato, began to be heard. It slid slowly upward in pitch and volume, and as it did, the dancers slowly turned to focus on center stage. There was a faint golden glow, slowly becoming brighter and brighter as the music rose, then out of the glow came a golden statue, a huge man, Hurkos, covered with gold paint, rigid. A piston kept lifting him until he was standing on a column above the heads of the dancers. Slowly he raised his arms; the dancers moved toward him, falling into a radial pattern focussed on the god. The god lifted his arms and the dancers drew nigh unto him. Suddenly he snapped his arms down and out, a great clash of cymbals, and the dancers began turning, whirling like dervishes, in complex geometric patterns like electrons around a nucleus. Brass and woodwind darted in and out, an individual dancer springing out of the swirling pattern momentarily as his instrument sounded, then back again as the tone stopped. Faster and faster went the dance, more and more complex, when suddenly there was the huge crash of all the instruments sounding at once, random, discordant, not like the end of Ravel's *Bolero* but truly random; there was a great bang of tympani, a great explosion of light in my eyes, the stage went completely dark, the music stopped abruptly, and I was left half-deaf, shaken, bright lights floating before my eyes.

The stage was dark for at least a minute, then the pattern began again. Now the dancers were wearing clothing: coarse shaggy fur kilts and skirts, loose fur vests closed by leather thongs, and flat leather sandals held to their feet by narrow criss-crossed lacing up their calves. The men wore large heavy fur hats held in place by chin straps; the women, bands of dyed fur around their foreheads. Crossed thongs outlined the women's breasts; crossed broad belts supported the short sword scabbard on each man's right side and the bare dagger on his left. The women wore colored fur wristlets on each hand, the men had broad leather braces on each forearm and narrower ones on each bicep. Each man had, wrapped around his waist, a wide strap made of plaited leather, and held by a huge golden D-shaped buckle.

The group was in a rectangular array, almost a static

crystalline mass. There was no music, just a beat, subtle at first, then becoming more and more insistent; a simple ominous deadening repetition on the kettledrum. Slowly the dancers moved, the women to the sides of the stage in two lines, the men toward the center, coalescing around one dancer, the Leader. He turned slowly and I could see it was Pierre Romanoff. A wave of applause swept the theater: love, respect, admiration, regret that he was retiring, although at forty-seven he was far beyond the age when a male dancer performed publicly in a lead role. Romanoff did not acknowledge the applause or break step, but continued forming the men into a loose military formation. Suddenly a spot snapped on, with the amplified twang of a metal string, showing the Ba'aal, golden and magnificent, dressed in gold military mail, with a large gold crown on his head. At once the tympani changed to a two-tone march rhythm, gradually accelerating. At the sight of the Ba'aal, the men stiffened and straightened their formation, taking on a sharp military look. Again the Ba'aal raised his hands; again he directed the dancers in their complex interweaving pattern, but this time the pattern was square, linear, right angled, and the women stayed on the outside, not mingling their movements with the men's.

Suddenly the men converged on the Ba'aal, who put out his hands. Each man unbuckled his plaited strap and placed the D-shaped gold buckle in the god's hands. Slowly the men made chainé turns outward, unrolling the belts from their bodies as they rotated, forming a huge circle over fifty feet across. The circle began to revolve and the drumbeat got faster and faster. As the wheel picked up speed, every second man began twirling, the wrapping of the belt around his waist pulling him in toward the Ba'aal. When these men reached the center, they began turning in the opposite direction, going outward again, while the other men began pulling inward. The giant wheel turned faster and faster, the dancers going in and out as it rotated. Hurkos' arm muscles stood out like cables; if he lost his grip the whirling men would fly out into the audience.

Then the drumbeat changed, and all the men were flying in and out together, the circle beating like a rotating heart, pumping and turning. Sweat was pouring off Hurkos; how much longer could he keep this up? The audience was stilled.

Flashes of bright golden light exploded toward the audience. Suddenly, when all the men were at the rim of the circle, a gong rang once. Each dancer leaped, twirling, into the air as the Ba'aal released his grip on the belt buckles. The belts came flying through the air, wrapping themselves around each dancer, the lights went out, the great discord sounded, and the audience burst into applause, for at least a minute, at the highest intensity.

Then a narrow golden spot snapped on from the rear of the theater, outlining the head of the Ba'aal. A single male dancer jumped in front of the god, his face catching the light at the top of his leap, a single slow drumbeat marking his jump. Two more drumbeats, two more jumps, then on the fourth beat he took a step forward. He jumped again, and behind him, a fraction of a second later, a second dancer's face caught the light. Four more beats and there were three dancers jumping, then four, five, six, until all fourteen men were leaping into the light, so that, as each face was lit up a tenth of a second after the one in front of him, it looked as though a bolt of lightning was drawn to, was striking, the god. For a dozen beats the line of men leaped with unbelievable precision, then the explosion of light in our eyes, the huge discord, and the stage went dark again. The applause was even louder and longer than before, and I applauded too. Modern or not modern, it was great.

The curtain went up again; a soft even blue light permeated the smoky air of the stage. The Ba'aal was seated on an executive chair, chrome and black plastic, in the middle of the stage. He was dressed in a black business suit made of scrim, so his golden body gleamed through when the light hit from the right direction.

The orchestra hummed like a beehive at a low intensity. One by one the male dancers walked on the stage, slowly, heavily, gracelessly, wearing black plastic business suits. Each went to the Ba'aal and handed him a golden ring that was attached to a thin golden cord. The Ba'aal put the rings on his fingers and sat quietly, hands in his lap. The men backed away from the Ba'aal slowly, to the limits of the golden cords attached to the golden ring on each one's right hand, forming a great circle, as before, but without life, without movement. The hum of the orchestra went on.

Slowly, the women, dressed in heavy soft black cloth, walked on stage, each dragging a smaller version of the Ba'aal's executive chair. Each went to a man and arranged the chair for him to sit facing the Ba'aal. Each woman handed her man a golden ring, which had a golden cord attached, to put on his left hand. She put the ring on the other end of the cord on her left hand and was then pulled sideways to the wings, pulled by the golden cord fixed to her right hand, by some offstage presence.

They all stayed in this position for a few seconds until a soft muffled drum roll began, an amplified metronome started a slow tick, and there came the ring of a clear little bell. Each time the bell rang, one of the men crumpled in his chair and fell to the floor. One by one they crumpled and fell.

When all the men were down, the Ba'aal rose and stretched his hands upward. He twitched gently at each man's string in turn, then all at the same time. No one moved. With a gesture of finality, he snapped his hands together, breaking all the golden cords. He stood for a moment, erect, defiant, then crumpled to the floor to the sound of a great C major chord played by the whole orchestra.

The curtain closed slowly and evenly as the audience went crazy with applause. Even Alexander, who never applauded out of politeness—"It just encourages them to put on more crap"—clapped hard and long.

Suddenly the curtain at the end of the box was ripped aside. It was Jeffrey Baron. "Dad! Dad!" he cried. "He's been killed!"

4

It was her kitchen table, so Julia Baron kept pushing *palatschinken* on us. I love the jam-filled crepes, but Alexander had already had three, which was three more than his *mehlspeise* quota for the day, and he looked as if he were ready to eat a dozen more.

"But we were going to have a party after the Gala," said Julia, "so nobody, I am sure, ate supper. Milk, eggs, flour, apricot jam, a little sugar, and a sniff of brandy. Perfect balanced diet."

Max Baron was silent, not eating, and his wife did not

urge him. She was clearly keeping the conversation going around him.

"Was it wise," asked Roberta, "to let Jeffrey talk to the police? Isn't it better not to say anything?"

"Burton is a very good attorney," Pearl said. "He won't let them do anything to Jeffrey."

"There was no way to avoid it," Alexander said. "If Jeffrey had refused to make a statement, he might have been charged."

"I'm sure Burton would not have allowed him to talk if there had been a better way," I said. "At least Burton is there with him. Think of the headlines if he had refused to cooperate: 'Billionaire Heir Shields Killer.' "

"You have a lot of influence, Pop," said Susan. "Why don't you just kill the whole deal?"

Max Baron winced at the words. "It is true, Susan, that I have influence, but it is not for such use. It would only make things worse if I tried."

"You have just to look at Jeffrey," said his mother, "to see that he could not kill anyone."

"No one said he killed anyone, Mommy," Roberta said. "All they want is information, and Jeffrey is the only witness."

"Baloney," Susan said. "The police are looking for a patsy, and Jeffrey is the only one who could have done it. Nobody could have gotten into Boguslav's box without Jeffrey's help. And besides, he hated the fat creep."

"Susan," her mother chided, "Jeffrey respected Mr. Boguslav."

The phone rang; Max Baron picked it up. He listened carefully, then said, "I want you to take care of this personally, Burton. Please." He nodded and hung up, turning to his wife. "Burton said they are going to charge Jeffrey in the morning." He took both of his wife's hands in his and said,

"I will do what has to be done." Mrs. Baron nodded at Alexander and said, "He is the right one."

Max Baron turned his chair toward Alexander. "Mr. Gold, I had intended to discuss with you another matter which, I understand, Burton has already mentioned." So Pearl had not made up the mind-reading bit. "It is much more urgent that my son be cleared of this crime he is accused of. Burton will do his job well in court, that I am sure of, but I do not wish for Jeffrey Baron to be even tried for murder. It is, therefore, necessary to show he is innocent so that there will be no trial. Can you do that, do you think?"

"Probably," Alexander replied. "But I have almost no information. After I get the facts I'll be in a better position to tell you."

"Burton has great confidence in you, Mr. Gold. He told me how you solved the Highland Steel embezzlement and how you found the murderer of Roger Allen Talbott. I would like you to undertake this project even with insufficient information. Please."

"What do you want me to do, Mr. Baron?"

"Free Jeffrey, please. With a clear name."

"To do that I may have to find the real killer."

"So. I see." Baron looked aside for a moment, then back to Alexander. "You are hinting, delicately, that I may not want the real killer found; that a member of my family may be responsible. Even myself."

"Anything is possible, Mr. Baron. Are you willing to take that risk?"

"It is not a risk, Mr. Gold. It is the dilemma of the Nazi asking the mother which child he should kill." Baron paused for a moment. "But you have not refused me outright, Mr. Gold. That means that you believe, as I do, that my son did not kill Viktor Boguslav. I know why I believe that, but what reason do you have to hold such a belief?"

"I saw him when he opened the curtain. That was not an act. He looked really confused and frightened."

"So. You would trust appearances, Mr. Gold?"

"Not alone, Mr. Baron. But as support, yes. You told Jeffrey I would be there, didn't you? And why?"

"Certainly. He was looking forward to talking to you at the party afterward. He loves to read detective stories."

"Then why would he deliberately pick a time and a place, when I was just a few feet away, to kill his boss? He must have had hundreds of better opportunities."

"That is a reasonable approach, but far from proof of his innocence. How certain are you, Mr. Gold, that Jeffrey is innocent?" Baron looked intently at Alexander.

"Jeffrey is innocent, all right," Alexander smiled confidently, "because the pattern isn't there. But the puzzle—Why in the box? Why during the performance?—that is not clear."

"Burton told me that you like puzzles, Mr. Gold; that you are very good at solving puzzles. And very fast."

"Well . . ." Alexander tried to look modest. Didn't succeed.

"Stop beating the bush around, Max," Mrs. Baron said. "Better plain talk now. Tell him what is on your heart. Everything."

Baron looked at his wife for a moment, then turned back to Alexander. He spoke very precisely. "I would like three things, Mr. Gold. Please. First, my son, Jeffrey, to be free, clear of all suspicion of the murder of Viktor Boguslav. Second, the Boguslav Ballet Russe to go on the Russian tour, which, if they do not leave on Sunday midnight, will be cancelled. Third, Jeffrey shall not go with them, and will leave the company, but not by force."

"The first and second are linked," Alexander said. "If I find the killer, the police would have no reason not to let the company leave. You must use your influence to cut the red tape, if required."

"For that, I can use my influence," Baron agreed.

"With Boguslav dead, whoever takes over . . ." Alexander was talking to himself, getting the feel of the probability of Jeffrey being not wanted as the new man's personal assistant. "I'll have to know personal things about your family, Mr. Baron. Will you cooperate fully?"

Baron looked at his wife thoughtfully. "Yes, Mr. Gold, fully."

"Only three days," Alexander was muttering to himself again.

"It will be worth your while, Mr. Gold."

"How much is that?"

"You must understand, Mr. Gold, that I cannot have a large number of people interfering with the police, making trouble, making bad publicity. I am betting all on you, no one else. I must have your maximum effort, concentrated, full time. I have found that large rewards are very helpful, but the possibility of loss is also very useful."

Alexander looked Baron straight in the eye. "Talk."

Baron stared back. "I will bet you one million dollars that you cannot accomplish these three things, against your one hundred thousand dollars."

Alexander, the big showdown hero, didn't flinch. "A month ago," he said, "I made a million dollars. After taxes and other little things, the income is barely enough to live on today. Tomorrow will be worse. Make it one million after taxes, Mr. Baron, and it's a deal."

"You are probably thinking that a million dollars is nothing to a billionaire, Mr. Gold, but you would be surprised how little my personal income is. Tax free it is. I will have Burton prepare the papers in the morning." He shook Alexander's hand, stood up, took his wife's hand and said, "It is late and we are all tired. The limousine will take you home. Susan, Roberta, you can stay, if you wish, tonight."

Roberta decided to stay, Susan to leave with us. Julia Baron showed us out, not wishing to wake the servants. At the door she took Alexander's face in her hands and said, "You will win. I know. I am never wrong. I am glad you made agreement with Max. He is sometimes hard to agree with for others."

I couldn't say what was on my heart in the limousine, and by the time we got home I decided not to risk a fight with Alexander. He had three days to solve a problem he knew nothing about, plus two other problems he knew even less about. He'd really have to knock himself out trying to find the killer before the deadline, go without sleep, eat badly, ruin his health, get panicky as the time approached . . . I could see it all now. Maybe even get the angina back. Or worse.

And where were we going to get the one hundred thousand if he failed? If we had to liquidate the investments we made last month, we'd be lucky to get half our money back. Then we'd be back to square one, worrying how to live in our old age.

I know why he did it too. He couldn't bear the idea that someone was so contemptuous of Alexander the Great, the super-genius detective who had just solved one murder case in a row; that the killer would have the audacity to commit murder only ten feet from Alexander Magnus Gold.

Alexander was going to make the killer pay for his *chutzpah*. I had a feeling I was going to suffer a bit too. I checked to see if we had enough Valiums in the house.

I decided we didn't.

5

"What else could the police do, under the circumstances?" asked Burton, over my perfect buttermilk pancakes. I had invited Pearl and Burton to have an early breakfast with us to give Alexander maximum use of every minute of the little time left.

"It sounds ridiculous," I said, "but with one sixth of the time gone, we still don't know anything about the murder other than what we saw, which was little enough. Get up and start pacing, Burton, I'll make more coffee."

Pearl went downstairs to Alexander's office to get the recorder. "Don't joke," Burton said, finishing his coffee, "I really think better when I'm addressing a jury, and the pacing helps." His voice changed. "Jeffrey pushed Boguslav into the box at about 7:15 PM and . . ."

"Pushed?" Alexander asked. "Why pushed?" Good grief, I thought, one hundred thousand dollars on the line and we don't even know fact one.

"Boguslav had broken both kneecaps," Burton said, "and was in a wheelchair. So it was Jeffrey's job, among other things, to push his boss around. Everybody knew that."

"In the ballet world, they knew," I said. "Not in the real world."

"How did Jeffrey get him up to the Grand Tier?" Alexander asked. "Wasn't Boguslav a big man?"

"Over three hundred pounds," Burton replied. "But there's an elevator that goes from the cellar to the First Balcony. Very few people know it exists; an early one with a round shaft, like the one a⁴ Cooper Union. Jeffrey made arrangements so it would be working last night."

"Where is it in relation to Boguslav's box?" Alexander asked.

"It opens on the fire stair landing at the end of the corridor, right next to the first box. All Jeffrey had to do was go through the stair exit door and make a left turn right into the box."

"Don't all fire exit doors have panic bolts?" Pearl asked. "So they can't be opened from the stair side?" She had become a panic bolt *maven* from the Talbott case.

"Yes, but Jeffrey had stuffed paper in the strike so he could open the door when he had to."

"We had to go down two steps from the corridor to our box," I said. "Was it that way for all the boxes?"

"Yes," Burton said. "And to answer your next question, Evan Spenser and Zoris Ziladiev, the ballet master, helped get Boguslav into the box. Jeffery is so skinny that if he had wheeled Boguslav down those steps alone, they both could have ended up in the orchestra pit."

"Did Spenser and Ziladiev leave right away?" asked Alexander.

"Right after they moved the wheelchair into position. Boguslav wanted to be exactly in the front corner of the box. Very fussy that it be done perfectly, as usual. They jockeyed him around while Jeffrey came to our box, and left as soon as Jeffrey got back."

"When was the curtain put up between our box and Boguslav's?" Pearl asked.

"The night before. Boguslav told Jeffrey to get it done, period. Jeffrey spent the night finding a curtain, getting it made to size, hooks installed, finding men to put it up. Don't forget there was nothing overhead to hang it from; a wooden framework had to be installed first. The next morning Jeffrey had to take Boguslav there to inspect it, to make sure it was done exactly the way he wanted it."

"Sounds like *El Exigente*," I said.

"You have no idea," Burton said. "Anyone running a ballet company has to be a bit of a dictator, but Viktor Boguslav wasn't called the Red Queen for nothing."

"Communist?" Alexander asked.

"Off-with-his-head type," Burton explained. "Anyway, after he was in place, Boguslav had Jeffrey stack all the chairs in the cloak area, so he could have the whole box to move around in, and close the curtain between the box and the cloak area. So Jeffrey arranged four chairs to stretch out and rest on, latched the door, and put out the light."

"Why couldn't Jeffrey sit in the box with Boguslav?" Pearl asked. "This way, he'd miss the ballet."

"Boguslav, I gathered, was not overly solicitous of Jeffrey's pleasure and well-being. He ordered Jeffrey to stay in the cloakroom, keep the curtain closed, and not bother him; he'd call Jeffrey when he needed him."

"No explanation?" I asked.

"Geniuses never explain."

"I always . . ." Alexander said, and we all laughed. "Well, I do," he said. Alexander's idea of an explanation is "It's obvious."

"How does latching the door help?" I asked. "It's just a flip-over little bar, like a public toilet latch. Anyone could slip a nail file through the crack and lift it."

"It would keep out idle visitors."

"Which way did Jeffrey set his four chairs?" Alexander asked.

"The only way he could: right across the entrance door, with the other chairs stacked against the wall at his feet."

"Were his feet pointing toward the stage or his father's box?" Alexander asked.

"Good point, Alec; I asked him that. His feet were pointing toward the stage, with the remaining four chairs stacked in pairs, one on top of the other, against the front wall of the box. The chairs he was lying on were set with their backs to the door. He arranged it that way so that when Boguslav wanted him, he could roll right out into the front of the box."

"Was he awake all the time?"

"He thinks he fell asleep shortly before the ballet started, but he doesn't know exactly when. He woke up just as *Graven Image* ended because he remembers hearing the last big chord and the applause."

"That was when he found Boguslav dead?"

"Yes. He felt guilty about falling asleep; afraid that his boss had called him and he hadn't answered. So he went into the box. Boguslav's wheelchair was in the same position they had left him, but his head was hanging back oddly. Jeffrey leaned over Boguslav's shoulder, the right shoulder, and saw the blood still flowing on his white blouse, and the knife—"

"The house lights were on?"

"No, but the stage lights were on full for the curtain calls, and Jeffrey could easily see everything."

"The blood was actually flowing?"

"He says yes, but it might have been his imagination. He was fatigued, thirty minutes sleep in the last thirty-five hours, imperfect illumination from the stage, looking over Boguslav's shoulder . . . Actually, there was very little blood on the shirt, but it still wet when Baron and Roberta climbed into the box and even several minutes later when the house security man came."

"What did the medical examiner say about the time of death?"

"Agrees with the circumstantial evidence; sometime after 7:30 and before 8:00 PM."

"During *Graven Image?*"

"We know Boguslav was alive at 7:20 or so. The house lights went out at 7:37 and the ballet started at 7:38 and ended about one minute to eight."

"Was there any chance anyone was hidden in the box before Boguslav got there?" Alexander asked.

"I wish there were," Burton sighed, "but with Jeffrey, Spenser, and Ziladiev in there maneuvering the wheelchair around, impossible. Nor could anyone have been hanging from the ceiling; there was no ceiling since the First Balcony does not extend over any of the side boxes."

"How about someone hiding in the cloakroom?" Pearl asked.

"With four chairs stacked and four spread out, and the light on, not even a midget could have been hiding there."

"Could someone have been hiding in our box and stepped over the divider just after Jeffrey closed the curtain?" Pearl asked.

"The timing was wrong," Burton answered. "We got there early. Roberta got Jeffrey just as Spenser and Ziladiev were moving the wheelchair around. Jeffrey was back before the other two left." Burton checked his watch and said, "I've got to meet Jeffrey and Max and go downtown. They're arraigning Jeffrey and I want to make sure he doesn't spend any time in jail. I'll call you when we're settled down at Jeffrey's."

As he left, I thought, with the simple logic Alexander likes, "If no one else could have been there, then only Jeffrey could have been the murderer." It was obvious.

6

I don't like looking at cold coffee, depressed husbands, and blondes who are desperately fighting the urge to say something cheerful, so I began thinking. To me, thinking is something you do afterward when your husband asks you why you did, instinctively, what you absolutely knew was the right thing to do *without* thinking—the mark of the truly bright person being the fast-lane synapse.

It didn't work. Naturally. To thine own self be true. So I made an agreement that when the second hand hit the twelve I would say something. It did and I did. "I know how he did it," I said. "How he got in. The killer, I mean." They looked at me, really surprised. I was surprised too. "The door. He opened the latch, not with a nail file, but with a knife. *The* knife. And let the latch down afterward the same way."

"But he couldn't open the door," Pearl objected. "Jeffrey's chairs were in the way."

"Not really," I said. "Jeffrey put his chairs against the step—remember, we had to step down into the box?—not against the door. How wide is a step, Alexander, about a foot?"

"About ten inches, give or take a half inch."

"There. Enough room for the murderer to get in, step over or around Jeffrey and the chairs, and kill Boguslav."

"There wouldn't be ten inches of room," Alexander said. "These were old-fashioned doors, heavy, almost two inches thick. And the backs of the chairs slope back a little. Figure about eight inches clearance between the door and the jamb, even if the killer could risk letting the door touch the chair, which might waken Jeffrey. Also, the doorknob sticks out two to three inches. And then he'd have to climb around a bunch of stacked chairs, all in the dark, without waking Jeffrey or alerting Boguslav."

"The killer could have ducked under the doorknob," I said. "And some of those ballerinas are real skinny, skeletons practically. They could fit."

"Why don't we check that?" Pearl said. "If we could show that it was possible, just possible, for someone to get into the box, Burton could use that to show reasonable doubt."

"Yes, let's measure," I said. "If a cat can get its head through a space, its whole body can get through."

"How about a midget?" Pearl asked.

"Or a child," I added. "There have to be children for the crowd scenes in *Petrouchka.*"

"And in the school," Pearl said. "There are always young girls in any ballet school, and they're all slim. Boys too."

"Why are we limiting ourselves to the ballet company?" I asked. "Couldn't anyone in the audience, or even in the theater, have been the killer?"

"No," Alexander said. "Obviously not."

"Again with the 'obvious,' Alexander?"

"Certainly. Boguslav was killed under extremely difficult circumstances in a practically locked room. Under conditions where it would take a good deal of luck not to be seen before, during, and after the deed. Even if we find a skinny little girl who could have squeezed her way into the box, would she have risked being seen by an usher or a passerby performing a very suspicious action? Much easier to kill Boguslav somewhere else. Besides, it wasn't a skinny little girl."

"It wasn't? You know?" Another Alexander 'obvious'?

"Just because we know," he said, "or believe that Jeffrey fell asleep, don't assume that everyone knows. It would have been logical to assume that Jeffrey would have been seated in the box with Boguslav. So our skinny little girl—assume a teenage student who has been betrayed by Boguslav, she decides to kill him, not in his bed when he's asleep, but in his box in front of a huge audience so she can become instantly famous—our girl has one little problem: As she's sneaking up on the impresario to stab him in the back—not in front because big strong Viktor might try to stop her—there is Jeffrey, trying to reason with her. On the other hand, if she tries to dispose of Jeffrey first, Viktor might hear him say 'ouch'—and no more big surprise for Viktor. Of course, little girls today are not as smart as they were before progressive education set in, and it is well known that all the oxygen goes to a dancer's feet, but still . . .''

"All right," I gave in. "Scratch the little girl. But there had to be some way for someone to get into the box without Jeffrey knowing. And out again."

"There was," he said glumly. "Remember what happened after Jeffrey called to his father?"

"Sure," Pearl said. "Max and Roberta stepped over the . . . Oh, my God!"

"Precisely," Alexander said. "That's why I asked Baron if he wanted me to find the real killer."

"But if you show that Baron, or even Roberta, stepped through the divider curtain, wouldn't that provide reasonable doubt as to Jeffrey's guilt?"

"No jury would believe," he answered, "that Jeffrey's fa-

ther or sister would kill Boguslav without Jeffrey's cooperation. Accessory before, during, and after the fact to premeditated murder is almost as bad as murder."

"They're both tall," I mused. "It might not have been
necessary to go into the box and implicate Jeffrey. Roberta,
especially, could have reached through the curtain halfway
into the box."

Pearl gasped. "Norma, that's horrible. Roberta would
never . . ., she's a . . ."

"Nice girl?" I finished. "Maybe she had an incentive no
nice girl could resist. We'll find out."

"How could she reach Boguslav?" Pearl asked. "He was
ten feet away."

"His foot was ten feet away, his head was four feet away,"
I pointed out. "Maybe he rolled the wheelchair over. Or
stood up. Even people with casts can move, if they hold on."
I turned to Alexander. "Shouldn't we check if he had crut-
ches or canes or something?"

"Wait," Pearl said. "Maybe the knife was thrown. If he
could stand up at the edge of the box, someone in the audience could throw a knife into his heart."

"From twenty feet below?" Alexander scoffed. "Without
anyone noticing? Not even the woman behind him whose
vision he was blocking? And how would he know when
Boguslav would stand up, if ever? No, Pearl, Boguslav was
killed by someone in, or adjacent to, his box."

"Julia Baron was holding her husband's hand all the
time," I said. "She would have noticed if he let go, and
certainly, if he moved the curtain to go into the next box,
the extra visibility of the stage would have been seen by all
of us."

"Not if the stage were dark," Alexander said, "and it was
dark several times, for long enough to kill ten men. If Max
took his hand away from his wife's for ten seconds, would

she notice? Or say anything if she did? Maybe if her son were on the way to jail, she might, not before."

"If the killing was done when the stage was dark, how did the killer find Boguslav?" I asked. "Or know where to stab him? With that lighting flashing in my eyes, there were times I couldn't see even when the lights were on."

"Maybe Boguslav used a penlight to take notes, or those sheets that glow in the dark," he replied. "We'll check what other source of illumination there was."

"Let's not leave Roberta," I said. "Susan wasn't holding her hand. Susan was probably not even watching the ballet. With those long legs, Roberta could step over the divider without showing her knees."

"They're a very loyal family," Pearl said, "in spite of the disagreements. If she thought she'd be believed, Julia Baron would confess to anything to save Jeffrey or her husband. Susan would do the same for Roberta."

"Why are we wasting all this time on conjecture?" Alexander said irritably. A bad sign, meaning he had no idea of even an approach to the solution. "We don't have any information at all, not about the people, not even about the knife. And you're both sitting around playing guessing games. Norma," he turned on me, "I want . . ."

"I already did it," I interrupted him.

"Did what?" he yelled. "I didn't even tell you what . . ."

"Stop yelling, Alexander," I said firmly. "I didn't put you in this stupid situation. I'm trying to help. I got up early this morning so you could get your full eight hours, and arranged everything. And you don't have to tell me what you want; I know already: reports on Boguslav and all his associates and friends; reports on the Barons; the layout and dimensions of the theater, the box, the entrances and exits; arrange an interview with Jeffrey; the works. It's all done."

He looked at me suspiciously. "You couldn't have. You

haven't made a call or a note since I got up; not one."

"There was no way Pearl or I could have done all this in less than a week," I answered, "so I called three research services, a building department expediter, a computer data information service, a clipping bureau, some friendly librarians—but I have to pay for the long-distance calls, two per diem researchers, and a reporter Pearl knows."

He looked overwhelmed. I continued, "Burton gave us several clerks and secretaries from his staff, who are right in his office now, starting to put the data and information together in an organized form. By this afternoon, Pearl will start putting some final drafts together and I'll do the editing and condensing. After supper—we're going to eat out, Chinese—you will have something to read; the rest you will get tomorrow morning. And I retained Lou Attell—he's a theater *maven*—to go to the theater and check measurements, trapdoors, and secret passages."

"You hired an engineer?" He turned red. "I'm an engineer!" he shouted.

"Not now, you aren't, darling." He deserved this, "Today you may be the General, or Hermann, or even Nick the Greek, but you're not an engineer. So shut up and play, genius."

He glowered, hates when I'm ahead of him, even as he appreciates it. "Do you know how much this will cost?"

"A lot less," I couldn't resist, "than one hundred thousand dollars, Mr. Bates." He either knew, or was afraid to ask, about the famous 'Bet-a-Million Bates.'

"What about Jeffrey? I have to talk to him."

"He'll be at home as soon as bail is set," I told him. "I arranged for Burton to call as soon as they get there."

"I don't want to talk to Jeffrey with his parents around."

"You won't," Pearl said. "Jeffrey has been living in Boguslav's house for the past three months."

"Are they—? No wonder Baron wanted Jeffrey out of the Boguslav. Why doesn't anybody tell me anything?"

"Pearl just did, darling," I said, "and maybe it's vice versa." He didn't laugh. I brought him his little case and said, "Take your vitamins and go for your walk, darling. Four miles today, congratulations, another milestone. No *noshing.* Pearl and I have to start organizing the files."

He had to have the last word. "I'll *think* while I walk." Implying that Pearl and I wouldn't. Well, with a big sixty-two hours to go, at least we knew what we didn't know: Everything.

7

From the outside, the Boguslav house looked like any other East Side brownstone, with only the ramp at the ground floor areaway to distinguish it. Inside—well!: an elephant-foot umbrella stand in the entrance hall, under a pair of crossed ivory tusks; a huge samovar on the buffet, encircled by tea glasses in silver holders, with a solid wall of ikons above; a pair of Texas longhorn horns set on a polished brass plate over a pair of crossed ancient muzzle-loader frontier rifles; all in a roomful of delicate Louis XIV furniture arranged on wall-to-wall bearskin rugs; the whole *mish-mash* making a surprisingly pleasant and comfortable room, as is so often the case when the householder follows only his own taste. Everyone compliments me on my home, how warm and friendly it feels, how felicitously the various elements complement each other. Yet it was never planned; I just bought the cheapest good-quality stuff I found that I thought Alexander would like.

The only disturbing thing, and I'm sure most people would never notice, was on the wall adjoining the dining room, and maybe it was *not* inconsistent with the rest of the room: a large old-fashioned framed canvas on which was spelled out in delicate, artistic needlepoint, embellished with Mexican motifs, the apothegm, "Con paciencia y saliva, un elefante se cogio una hormiga." I felt sure that the old maiden-aunt type who had been conned by Boguslav into taking her eyes out for a month copying the words did not know that what she had so carefully transcribed said, "With patience and spit, an elephant screws an ant," and "screws" is a euphemism.

Jeffrey, seated opposite the couch, looked somewhat more relaxed than when we had met him, but he still kept looking toward the stairs as though expecting a summons from his dead employer.

"I made a deal with the DA," Burton said. "In return for not arraigning Jeffrey now, Jeffrey made a full statement and will not leave Manhattan."

"I thought you advised all your clients to say nothing," Pearl said.

"The DA was going to hold Jeffrey as a material witness. Jeffrey would have had to talk, and anything he said could not have made things look any worse than they are now. Or so I thought," he added resignedly.

Alexander jumped right in. "Jeffrey Baron, did you kill Viktor Boguslav?"

"No, sir," Jeffrey answered.

"Did you have anything to do with his murder, or help in any way, or know who did it? Or suspect?"

"No, sir."

"Do you know why he was killed, or have any idea?"

"Well, Mr. Gold, he was a little difficult to get along with. Most people didn't understand him."

"Or like him, Jeffrey?"

"Some people loved him." Jeffrey showed some life.

"You, for one?"

"I respected him, Mr. Gold. I admired what he had accomplished."

"How did you become his personal assistant?"

Jeffrey leaned forward in his chair, his posture a plea for understanding. "I've always loved the ballet, but I didn't have the body for it. Not that I couldn't have made the *corps de ballet* if I stuck it out, but I had to be very good or nothing. My father always set very high standards for us, but we couldn't . . . Roberta might, but Susan and I . . . He wanted me to train to take over his business."

"He pressured you?"

"Max Baron never pressures. He says 'please' and makes it so desirable for you to do what he wants that you want to do it as badly as he does."

"What did he offer you?"

"Work in a small business for five years, anywhere, where I could learn. Work with him the next five years to learn how he did things. At thirty-five I would either take over the business, or become head of the Foundation. If I didn't want either, or he felt I could not handle either job, he would give me one million dollars. To start a business, to waste, whatever I wanted. After that I would get no more money as long as he lived or my mother lived. She's a lot younger than he is."

"There are many people who would give a lot for such an

opportunity," Alexander said quietly. I was sure he was thinking of his own father who, when Alexander was a boy, lost his little store for lack of fifty dollars.

"Oh, I took it," said Jeffrey. "I'm no fool. But the business I selected was running a ballet company. That way I could do what I loved and still fulfill my father's requirements. Fortunately, the fellow who used to be Mr. Boguslav's personal assistant had just resigned, bought into a taxi fleet, and I happened to be in the right place at the right time and Mr. Boguslav hired me."

"Is the Foundation a big contributor to the Boguslav Ballet?"

Jeffrey jumped to his feet, his face red. "People are always saying that. It isn't true. I was hired on merit. The Foundation always contributed to the Boguslav and I was never hired before. I work very hard and I always accomplish what I'm told." He sat down, glowering.

"Like the curtain between the boxes, Jeffrey?" Alexander probed gently.

"Exactly. Right after supper he told me to get it done, and by next morning it *was* done, exactly the way he wanted. Do you have any idea what it's like to find a curtain maker and a carpenter in New York at night? Damn few people could have done it."

"Had he ever had a curtain like this put up before?"

"Not while I was with him. Probably not ever before. I asked him where the curtain was so I could have it installed. He said there was none."

"Must have been expensive, Jeffrey."

"I spent over a thousand dollars."

"You spent?"

"The company will reimburse me."

"What is your salary, Jeffrey?"

"Salary? I should really *pay* Mr. Boguslav for the educa-

46

tion I'm getting. I just pay for my room and board here."

"To the company?"

"I make out the checks to Mr. Boguslav and he uses them for company requirements." And this baby was going to take over a billion-dollar business empire in ten years? God help America. To hell with solving the murder; let the little *yold* hang. My problem was how to get adopted by a billionaire.

"So, Jeffrey, Boguslav was a demanding employer?"

"He had to be, Mr. Gold. He ran the company practically single handed. He was artistic director, general manager, and fund raiser; he hired and fired; he took care of publicity, advertising, and public relations; he arranged the contracts, the leases, the bookings, the tours; took care of the union problems; he sat in on class and rehearsals and made notes on the performances. He was a superman."

"Not all the members of the company appreciated this?"

"Well, Spenser felt he was the best judge of the music. And Ziladiev thinks that he alone should run the class and rehearse the ballets as *régisseur*. Of course, Pierre, especially now, hates when someone criticizes his technique; he used to be the greatest, the best in the world, and even today, he's still quite good."

I had been looking forward to seeing Romanoff do *Petrouchka*. Maybe, at his age, he didn't have the *ballon* anymore, but what an actor, what a great actor. Near the end of the ballet, when the Moor kills Petrouchka, when the little doll collapses to the floor as a heap of sawdust, his temporary magical life ebbing from the limp body, there isn't a dry eye in the house. And I have heard sobs in the theater when the Charlatan picks up the limp rag doll to show that it never could have lived or loved, and flings the now empty shell away.

I have seen many *Petrouchkas,* but the greatest of them

all, and don't tell me about Nijinsky, is Pierre Romanoff. He can tear your heart apart with a single gesture.

I hated the murderer for this alone: A decent one would have waited until the show was over. Or, at least, *Petrouchka.*

"Any other little frictions, Jeffrey?" Alexander asked.

"The usual, same as in any other company. Tatiana doesn't want Betsy around, says she's a troublemaker, especially now. Tatiana was really upset at Boguslav for picking *Gala Performance* for the final show."

"Because there are three *prima ballerinas* in it?"

"Naturally. She's been *prima* for a lot of years, she's not about to share that with anyone. And what's worse, he picked this ballet for Boruskaya's first American appearance after her defection. No one will even look at Tatiana. Betsy is mad because she thinks she's a better dancer than Tatiana and Irina put together and wants to be *prima ballerina.* And Kurt Tindall threatens to go to the Stuttgart unless he is featured in the ads as *premier danseur.*"

"Is there anyone in the company who liked Boguslav?"

"You're not supposed to *like* him, Mr. Gold," Jeffrey said. "And, yes, the *corps de ballet* didn't hate him, just the usual complaints: not enough money, costumes too tight to move in, slippery spots on the stage, having to wear the shoes too long, that sort of thing. Nothing serious."

"Why did you hate him, Jeffrey?" Alexander slipped in quietly.

Jeffrey got red again. Boy, would I like to get him in a poker game. Or even bridge. "Who said I hated him? Was it Tindall? Well, I know why he said that. It's not true. I didn't hate him. I felt that Mr. Boguslav was a very capable individual who was performing a very difficult job quite well, under the circumstances, with some extremely uncooperative people."

"But when you take over the company," Alexander smiled confidently, "you'll do things a little differently."

"Of course I will—would," Jeffrey corrected quickly. "It's only logical that I carry on, for the while, until the company gets a new general manager. I'm the only one who knows what's going on at all levels, in all areas."

"But you can't do this if you're in jail for murder . . ."

"I didn't kill . . ."

"And if the company doesn't go on the Russian tour it will lose everything and . . ."

"We *will* go; we *have* to . . ."

"The company will fall apart all because you killed your homosexual lover!" Alexander shouted right into Jeffrey's face.

"I didn't," he screamed. "Pierre is lying. I never. I'm not! Pierre is. Everybody says I am but I'm not. Even my father . . ." He burst into tears.

Pearl ran to hold him. Burton got up heavily and looked at Alexander gravely. "You should go now, Alec," he said. "There's nothing more to learn here, especially now, in his condition: no sleep, his boss killed in front of him, arrested for murder, his family upset. Let him sleep. I'll talk to him later."

"And tell me what he said?" Alexander was suspicious.

"Unless it's privileged," Burton said.

"I must know everything, Burton, otherwise I can't function. Max Baron promised to cooperate with me. Check with him. Tell him that I want full cooperation from everyone, and full information. I want him to use his influence, and you to use yours, to get me a copy of the medical examiner's report. And the complete police file. Steal it if you have to; bribe someone, I don't care, but get me what I need. I mean it, Burton. Tell Baron if I don't get everything I need, the bet is off; I'll just walk away."

Alexander? My Alexander saying, even hinting, that he would quit a game before the end? Even a game that was stacked against him? Alexander never gave up. Never. That was how he lived through the heart attack. Maybe he was trying to tell me something. Such as "start worrying."

I didn't need to be told.

Fifty-eight hours left.

•

8

Alexander was in his premenstrual state: That is the state he gets into when I am premenstrual. So I sent him upstairs to do ten miles on his stationary bicycle with strict orders to take a warm bath and a two-hour nap afterward.

Pearl was checking the early returns from our researchers, so I returned the calls on my machine. "No trapdoors, no secret passages, no catapults, and no mirrors on the ceiling," Lou Attel reported. "But the place is wide open; I could take an army through there undetected. Anybody who can push a button can take that elevator, it's slow but it gets there, from the cellar to the Orchestra to the Grand Tier to the First Balcony. The fire stairs run from the cellar to the roof, and that includes the outside fire escapes."

"Are you telling me," I asked, "that anybody could get to Boguslav's box?"

"From anywhere in the theater *to* anywhere in the theater in five minutes. There are exit stairs and doors at the front, middle, and rear of the house and where the Second Balcony doesn't reach, there is a fire passage to the front and middle stairs. The Phantom of the Opera could have raised his grandchildren there in perfect privacy."

"Alexander is going to want the dimensions around that box, Lou."

"I'm a pro, Norma; I got them. The box is nine feet, six inches by six feet, one inch clear inside. The front and end walls are eleven inches thick and three feet high, topped with a velvet-covered three-inch-diameter pipe rail extending up eight inches more. Two stub partitions, five-and-a-half inches thick and two feet long, separate the box from the rear area; a pair of heavy velvet curtains can close off the front. The rear area is the same length as the front, by three feet, six inches deep. You enter by a right-hand swing door, nominally three feet wide, centered in the corridor wall. The box is fifteen inches down from the corridor, with two seven-and-a-half inch risers, of which the bottom tread is ten inches wide."

"Got it on tape, Lou. Where is the box door in relation to the stair and the stage?"

"The outside wall of the fire stair is in line with the end of the box, so the doorknob to the box is three feet, six inches from the fire stair. The outside face of the end wall of the box is two feet, eight inches from the edge of the stage and the back of the box is exactly in line with the face of the proscenium arch. The proscenium is twenty-four inches thick to the house curtain, and the stage extends three feet, four inches in front of the proscenium, overhanging the orchestra pit by nineteen inches."

"What about elevations?" I asked.

"The stage is three feet, nine inches above the orchestra

floor and there are six risers down from the stage to the Orchestra. The bottom of the box is sixteen feet, four inches above the Orchestra floor, and the floor of the box is eleven inches thick, finish to finish."

"If someone wanted to throw a knife from the orchestra," I added up the dimensions, "he'd have to throw upwards twenty feet, three inches minus the height of his shoulders. Right, Lou?"

"No," said Lou. "You're forgetting that the shoulder heights almost cancel out, unless the victim got stabbed in the toes. You also forgot the railing, so it's really about twenty-one feet above the orchestra. But you're assuming the victim was leaning over the rail. If he were standing straight up at the railing, there would have to be an angle of throw, so the actual flight of the knife might be twenty-one feet vertical and maybe ten feet horizontal, so figure a path about, um, twenty-four feet."

I had been sketching as he spoke, and suddenly it struck me. "How wide is a chair, Lou?"

"Depends. Anywhere from fourteen to twenty inches. Could be more. You didn't tell me to measure the furniture."

"I know, Lou. Here's what I have in mind. Say the chairs are eighteen inches wide; if you put four of them together, that's six feet. The opening edge of the door is six feet, three inches from the end of the box. That means the door to the box could have been opened wide enough for the killer to slip in, even if Jeffrey were sleeping on the chairs."

"Sure," Lou said. "If it was set up that way even Alex could get through. But it wasn't. A man goes to sleep, he puts one chair under his head, one under his shoulders, one under his hips, and one under his feet. How tall was the kid?"

"Six even, roughly. But he wouldn't put the chair under

his feet, he'd put it under his calves. Try it several ways, Lou, but I'll bet that if you set the edge of the first chair tightly against the end wall, you can open the door enough for someone to slide in."

"You may have something there, Norma. I'll go back and try it. Call you in a couple of hours."

Well! Alexander should be pleased at this development. Miffed, too, that I figured it out, but tooooo bad. And he'd have to give me the credit in front of everybody. I'd check with Jeffrey later to find out how he actually placed the chairs and how sound a sleeper he was. Now that there was a way to get into the box, we wouldn't have to sell our tax exempts. I felt a lot better as I returned Baron's call.

"I called to see if there was anything you required," he said.

"No progress yet, Mr. Baron, if that's what you really called about, but there is plenty you can do. We need all the information the police have, especially the medical examiner's report, and we need it now. If Burton needs help, influence . . ."

"I will call some people," he said confidently.

"Then you and your wife are to be here at five o'clock today. Alexander wants to question each of you."

He hesitated for a moment, then said, "He is wrong, but I understand his need. You said 'each.' If that means separately, it cannot be done. My wife and I speak as one. We will be there at five."

"I need Susan's and Roberta's phone numbers, and you to tell them to talk to us."

"Why do you involve the girls, Mrs. Gold?"

"I didn't, Mr. Baron. Jeffrey did."

He gave me the numbers and a promise the girls would cooperate. They were both home, Susan sounding as though she had just gotten up. Susan lived on the West Side, near us, Roberta on the East Side. I took Roberta, figuring even

Pearl could handle Susan. "And turn on your recorder this time," I reminded Pearl. Alexander believes the first mistake can be due to stupidity, the second is because you hate him. We didn't have time for Alexander to give Pearl a two-hour lecture, even though it would have done her much good.

9

While Roberta was making coffee, I checked her bookshelves: philosophy of science, statistical methods, stochastic interaction, romantic novels, Cavalier poetry, and how-to-catch-a-man. I felt like crying. This is what would have happened to me if I hadn't been lucky enough to meet Alexander.

Roberta served good coffee, even though she lived on the East Side. In a simple green dress, with her long auburn hair loose, she looked like an ad for *House and Garden*. "I'm working on photosynthesis," she said. "One little corner. Studying the chain of interactions—it's an extremely complex process—or rather, one tiny link in the chain. There's a protein in spinach that seems to be a key unit in the process. Call me Roberta."

"What's a nice girl like you doing in a field like that, Roberta?"

"The Institute started the project. It looked interesting,

well funded, and it could really help the food problem. If we could produce photosynthesis *in vitro,* or even increase photosynthetic activity a little, it could be the salvation of mankind." (A Nobel Laureate with a forty-six D bosom? That would put the filthy little beasts in their place.)

"I see you jog," I said, pointing to the shoes in the corner.

"Weekends and holidays. I have a tendency to gain weight, and jogging helps. Also, I like to be in the park."

"You jog alone?"

"I prefer to. Besides . . ." She stopped and, I swear, blushed.

"Besides, all your friends are much shorter and you think it makes you look like an elephant," I said bluntly.

She began to cry. I let her, for a while, then put my arms around her. "Roberta, I said that purposely. Not to make you feel bad, but to get it out of the way. Because that's the way you really feel about yourself, and you're wrong. I know. I'm almost as big as you are, and much heavier, so I can say it. That was the way I felt when I was eighteen, and even after I was married I felt that way for many years. Thank God, my husband is so conceited he thinks he is bigger than I am, if he ever noticed at all."

She stopped crying and began listening. "When I met Alexander," I told her, "he wasn't handsome; he was even a little unusual looking, but he was a man. Even then, at twenty-two. A little crazy in some ways, but honest, straight, manly, strong. I knew right then he was my man. I was only eighteen, but I was a woman, not a girl. I had responsibilities, I had duties, I had ambition, I had promise. But what I really wanted was to be a wife. His wife."

"What happened?" Roberta asked. "You married him, obviously."

"Yes, certainly, that's why I'm telling you this. So you can learn from my experience. I met him on a Friday night. We spent the whole Saturday together. Everything from my first impression was true; the good was better than I thought, the bad was worse. A balance. I didn't care; I was sure. On Sunday, we went to the beach. I arranged it so we stayed late, after dark. Then I led him under the boardwalk and seduced him."

"Was it good?"

"If you mean did I have an orgasm, no. But it was good. It was loving, uniting, completing, like a seal on a contract, like the logical conclusion."

"Were you a virgin?"

"In those days everybody was a virgin. Some people didn't even make love before they were married."

"Did it bother you?"

"Not a bit. I was proud and happy. I even told my mother. Because he was the man for me. Exactly for me. Made in heaven, just for me."

"It sounds so beautiful."

"It will happen to you, I know it. Anyway, one week later I told him we were going to get married. Just told him. You know what he said? Not 'I don't want to get married'; not 'But I hardly know you'; not 'I just wanted to get laid, not married.' No, none of these. My romantic hero, my dashing Cavalier, just said, 'We can't afford it yet.' I was in seventh heaven."

"Why? He just refused to marry you."

"He did not refuse; he accepted. The only obstacle was money."

"Did you have money?"

"Of course not. Nobody had money. So what? You think I would let a little thing like money stand in my way? I transferred to night school and got a job. I transferred him to day school so he could get his degree quicker. Simple. We got married right after the end of the semester."

"And lived happily ever after," Roberta concluded.

"No. That's fairy tales. Mostly happily, sometimes unhappily, but always interesting. And always with love. That's what will happen to you, Roberta, for sure. But the point I'm making is, you have to do it yourself. If you wait for some idiot man to do something you'll end up an old maid."

"I'm trying. I really am."

"You're not. When you're jogging, do you ever go up to a man and talk to him?"

"It's very hard to do. He could be married; you can't tell by looks."

"I can; you'll learn. Meanwhile, do this. Leave your hair down, it's really beautiful. Lose ten pounds; by exercise, not by dieting. Wear your contacts whenever you're out of the house. And change your job; get one where you meet people. And the next man you meet who acts like a man, invite him out, take the initiative."

"I'll wear the contacts and lose the weight. And leave my hair down. I'll even try to take the first step if I meet a nice man. But I don't think I could . . . I do good work at the Institute and I like it."

"Okay, four out of five. Now," I said abruptly, "did your father climb through that curtain? Did he kill Boguslav?"

Roberta looked shocked. "If you knew my father, you wouldn't even ask that. He never in his life . . . He is incapable of hurting anyone. Even psychologically. He can't, literally can't, cause anyone pain."

"Suppose someone hurt you. Or Susan. Or Jeffrey."

She stiffened and looked behind her, as if for help. She would not look at me. "He would tear that person to pieces with his bare hands. Mommy made us, when we were little, never to tell him, only her."

"What if someone hurt your mother?"

She was silent for a long time. I waited. Finally she said, "My father would sacrifice all of us, even Jeffrey, for my mother."

"So. Did your father climb through that curtain?"

"I didn't feel the curtain move, even once."

"You weren't sitting touching the curtain, Roberta, I saw you. You were far to the right, so you could see better."

"I would have seen the curtain move against the stage light."

"There were several periods of total darkness, some lasting for a minute or two. Long enough to kill a man," I said harshly.

"Your reasoning is wrong, Mrs. Gold. If my father wanted to kill Viktor Boguslav, would he have done it in such a way as to implicate Jeffrey?"

"Sure he would," I said, feeling like an executioner, "you said so yourself. If Boguslav had hurt your mother."

She started sobbing quietly. "Did you know Boguslav?" I asked. She nodded. "Did your mother?" She didn't move, just looked up at me piteously.

I left her crying. Score one for us good guys.

10

Pearl was already in the office, transcribing her interview with Susan Baron. "Anything good?" I greeted.

"Oh sure," she said. "There are major clues that you and I overlooked completely. Would you believe that the end dancer on the left in the first scene has a bigger bulge in his leotards than even Danilo Hurkos?"

"Nope, I missed that. Got distracted with all that dancing going on. Did you inform Little Miss Crotchwatcher that some of these *boychicks* stuff stockings into their codpieces to overwhelm their admirers? Who are not necessarily of the female persuasion? Seriously, did she see anything useful?"

"I don't think she hears too well in the soprano register, but I did put a few questions to her in my deepest growl. I got the impression that if Roberta had been eaten by two grizzly bears, Susan might have taken her eyes off the bulges for a second. One bear, I'm not too sure."

"What about during the dark periods?"

"Best time for fantasizing."

"Did you tell her there were girls on the stage too?"

"You'll never convince her; she knows what she saw."

Fun is fun, but it was almost time for the Barons to arrive. I debated whether or not to edit the cassette of my interview with Roberta, but what the hell, let Alexander get the flavor of this girl so he would understand why I didn't ask her if *she* had climbed through the curtain.

I took the recorder up to the bedroom with a cup of tea to ease the shock of waking up. He listened as he dressed; his only comment was, "Why did you lie to her? You know that I decided to marry you the moment I saw you." He really believes it; with loving words I do not argue.

When I invited the Barons to sit down, Max moved his chair so he could sit right next to his wife. "Pearl is working on the Boguslav Report," I told them. "Since you see her socially, I felt you could answer personal questions more freely if she were not here."

"That is considerate of you, Mrs. Gold," Baron said. "To carry it to the logical conclusion, would it not be better if we spoke to Mr. Gold only? Please?"

"My wife and I are one," Alexander said. "Trust me, trust her."

"Good," said Julia Baron, taking her husband's hand. "That is the way it should be. So. What do you want to know, Mr. Gold?"

"What is the relationship," Alexander asked, "between the Foundation and the Boguslav Ballet Russe?"

"We provide fifty percent of their budget," Baron said.

"Was that how you forced Viktor Boguslav to take your son, Jeffrey, as his personal assistant?"

"Why do you have such a low opinion of Jeffrey, Mr. Gold?" Alexander kept silent. After a moment Baron continued. "The Foundation gives money according to the principles of Maimonides; we never interfere with the operations of our beneficiaries."

"How much did it cost you personally, Mr. Baron?"

Baron hesitated. "I have always felt, Mr. Gold, that a young man should have at least one door opened to him, to have the opportunity to fulfill a dream. Otherwise, his whole life he will wonder for what might have been." Alexander waited. "Forty thousand dollars. I did it on my own, without consulting—anyone." Still silence. "I gave it to Boguslav personally, not the company."

"And Boguslav's previous assistant, Mr. Baron? The one who bought into the taxi fleet?"

"He was going to leave anyway; he was not happy with Boguslav." Again, silence. Baron went on. "Susan is not qualified. Roberta is not interested. Jeffrey is my only son." Max Baron's accent grew more pronounced. He spoke jerkily. "I have built an empire from nothing. Many thousands of people dependent on me. Neither Julia nor I have anyone besides ourselves and the children. The managers of today —they would close down a plant without a thought, to increase profit this year only by one-tenth point. For this they would destroy families, lives, industries. For the future they care nothing; not builders, they harvest what other people have planted. Jeffrey is not stupid, just young. If he had not done this, he would forever be—discontent. Like to fail to marry the right girl when the time came."

"For you to offer the money to Boguslav," Alexander said, "you had to know he was a crook. Why would you want your son under his influence?"

"Boguslav, you should understand, was a brilliant man; strong, dedicated, he loved the ballet more than life. He built the company from nothing too; held it together by himself. Not since Wassily de Basil could this be done. The same principles to run a ballet as a business empire are necessary; Jeffrey could learn much from Boguslav. And yes, I knew Boguslav was dishonest. Not a crook, he was not trying all the time to steal, just that he would do anything to keep the company alive; things you would not do, but which I would do to keep my organization alive. And he succeeded. For twenty years *he* was the Boguslav Ballet Russe. That is something. And I too am dishonest, Mr. Gold. If he took, I gave; but I hoped to produce good and, I am sure, so did he."

Alexander wisely changed tack. "The tour of Russia, Mr. Baron. If any company were to go, should it not have been the New York City Ballet again?"

"It should not and it could not, Mr. Gold. True, they have great dancers, a great school: Balanchine, Robbins, everything better than the Boguslav. They are rich, endowed, have their own theater. Balanchine wants to spend thousands extra to have *real* silk gowns for *Vienna Waltzes,* he spends it. And he is right; when you see how the gowns flow with the dance . . . it is so beautiful, perfection. Like the Russian companies: You want 100 in the *corps de ballet* on stage, you have it; you want an orchestra of one hundred and twenty players, you have it; you want whatever you want, tell the commissar; the government pays. So if City Ballet goes to Russia you are comparing practically one collective with another. Two giants; one dances this way, one the other way. Americans better at this, Russians better at that. You could like both.

"But, the commissars think, maybe the Russian people will like the Americans better. This cannot be allowed. So, the Boguslav, Mr. Gold, the Boguslav. Small, poor, weak, one man, capitalist, not collective. Same ballets as the Russians: no Balanchine, just Fokine, Petipa, Ivanov. There will be no American advantage having Balanchine's choreography. With the Boguslav and the Russians dancing the same ballets, same choreography, equal comparison, the Russians must win. No competition. How can the poor weak Boguslav, even some American critics make fun of, be next to the Kirov, the Bolshoi. The Americans will look like poor relatives, shabby, not even in the same class; the Russian people would see and compare; they would see the Russians are better. So the commissars do not fear the Boguslav. The KGB types they send to check up, what do they know? They see the small company, the old scenery, the worn costumes . . . They report back: It is safe to take the Boguslav. How can KGB know of beauty, of soul, of freedom? So the tour is arranged."

"How did you arrange it, Mr. Baron?" Alexander asked.

"Simple. I give them everything. The Foundation—for once I use my influence on the board of directors—pays for everything, even the living accommodations, to the Russians. The company must fly Aeroflot, must bring dollars, must hire Russian musicians, must spend, spend, spend; minimum three million dollars. So the Russians get their favorite game: to make America and the capitalists look bad and make the Americans pay for the privilege. This they could not refuse."

"It's well known that you hate the Russians. Why do this for them?"

"Some Russians I hate, and all communism. But maybe there will be a surprise when they see the Boguslav Ballet Russe: how good they are, how beautiful, how much joy, how much heart; how free people dance. Maybe the Russian people will learn from art what is possible to be done without government, without commissars, without chains, without camps."

"And one thousand Jews," said Julia Baron.

"Yes," Max Baron said. "I strike a bargain. When all else is agreed, when the commissars cannot easily go back to the dictator and say deal is off, I say let one thousand extra Jews go. It costs them nothing, they can take the credit. Otherwise no deal. They agree."

"The Russians do not always keep their word, Mr. Baron. After the Boguslav has a triumphal tour, and the Russians feel they've been sandbagged, after you stir longings for beauty and freedom in the hearts of ten thousand Russians —suppose the commissars reneg? What then?"

"I am aware of this, Mr. Gold, and they could do it. But it would become known, and they would lose much credibility in their business deals with the West, which they so desperately need. So I think they will let the thousand go. But we have to be careful, exact in our dealings. There are commissars who do not want to let us in, or anyone out. That is why we must leave exactly at midnight on Sunday. Otherwise, all falls apart."

"How could we not take the opportunity," Julia Baron asked, "to free one thousand people? Even if it will fail, still we must try."

Alexander looked from Julia Baron to Max and back to Julia again. He seemed to choose his words carefully. "Have you ever rolled up your sleeves, Mr. Baron, during a business meeting? Do you always, Mrs. Baron, wear long-sleeved dresses?"

There was a long silence, then Julia Baron spoke, her soft blue eyes cold. "When we could afford to have the numbers removed, we decided not to. But not to show others, even the children. For ourselves. What changed once can change again. We live, always, without possessions to bind us in a place. In five minutes, if we have to, I put in my pocket everything I love, leave all else behind, and run. Everything fixed they can take away from you, even what is in my pocket. But if we are together, they have nothing and I have everything."

Max Baron stared into the distant past. "I met my wife, for the first time, the day the Nazis ran away. The Russians, it was rumored, were only twenty kilometers away. Everyone, those of us who were still alive, broke into the stores and ate. We waited for the Russians to save us; it was not safe for Jews in the middle of Poland. Julia came in the storeroom and I knew. Right away I knew. I gave her bread and we talked. I did not know then that she would look so beautiful, that was later. She said, 'Get a sack. Put in food. We must run, escape.' I said, 'Why? The Russians will come here tomorrow. They will take care of us.' But she said we must go. I could not let her go without me. But I could not go together with a young girl, she was sixteen, I was twenty-eight, all alone. So I said, 'You must marry me. I will not touch you. When we are safe, if you wish, we will divorce.' I loved her, but I would have kept my word."

He paused and took a deep breath. "There was a rabbi in the camp, very old. He had kept himself alive because he was needed; now he was dying. He married us, it took only a few minutes, and we went away. I wanted to go east, she said southwest. I agreed. Of all the others in the camp, I never heard of even one again. Siberia, dead . . . who knows.

"We walked. Each time we came to a fork, she said, 'this way' or 'that way.' I wanted to find the Partisans; she said no. Later we found some Partisans killed Jews; we were lucky. Then we found the Americans. They gave us food, work, clothing, a bed. We worked. Hard. They even gave us money and helped us come to this golden land. The rest is in the records. It is not completely inaccurate. You Americans do not appreciate freedom, how good it is here. We do."

"My husband," said Julia Baron, "has a poor memory. Purposely. When I saw him, he was so beautiful, so strong, so wise, I wanted him to love me, protect me. I wanted to make my life with him. I made him marry me and I knew that we would never part, even when we were safe."

Alexander's voice was gentle. "You saw so much brutality, Mr. Baron. How did it affect you?"

"You are asking roundabout questions again, Mr. Gold. Under certain, very limited, conditions, I could bring myself to kill, yes. But I did not do it."

"You are rich enough to get others to do anything for you."

"I do not ask of others what I should do myself."

"What if Boguslav were bringing harm to Jeffrey?"

"I am competent to stop a situation without murder."

"If Boguslav had already harmed your son? Irreparably?"

Julia Baron spoke up quickly, before her husband could answer. "If I thought that Max might kill a Boguslav, I would kill him first myself, so that Max would be spared the torture. And I am stronger than Max—don't shake your head, Max—and I would see it first before he even knew, and it would be done before Max even realized he was going to *think* of killing."

Alexander smiled wryly. "Would you say anything differently if you were sure Jeffrey did it?"

"Certainly," she smiled. "You will know Jeffrey did it when I confess I did it." She stood up. "Come, Max. We are wasting Mr. Gold's time. He has work to do."

As soon as they left, Alexander came to me and took me in his arms, tightly. He was crying. I didn't have to ask why. But I had to say what was on my heart. "He didn't do it, Alexander. I know that. But what do we do if she did it?"

11

Just as we were going out to eat, Lou Attell called. Before he started, I said, "About throwing the knife, Lou, we never considered doing it from the stage. That's almost four feet higher, so it should be easier to do."

"Are you kidding?" he sneered. "With all those lights on and a thousand people watching?"

"How about when it was dark?"

"Good trick, Norma. Memorize where he should be, hope he doesn't move, run to where you think you should be, throw, and zap, you've killed the conductor."

"Is it possible or not, Lou?"

"Not. Positively not, even if the victim was standing up. There is not enough room horizontally to be at the right angle. The curtain is only eight feet from the front of the box."

"What if he stood in back of the curtain?"

"Come on, Norma. A theater curtain is a lot bigger than you think it is; weighs tons and bulks up several feet wide in the open position. The proscenium is in line with the end of the box and the curtain is kept closed about six feet wide when the show is on. If the killer stood far enough back to have the proper angle, he'd most likely stab the curtain rather than the victim."

"What if he threw left-handed?"

"That would help the angle, but he'd have to move closer to stage center to even see the box, and that would increase the distance of throw. And in the dark, too."

"Well, it was a thought. Back to the chairs, Lou."

"In the most favorable position," he said, "the door to the box leaves a space of nine and a quarter inches, not counting the doorknob, which is easy to duck under."

"That's all?" I couldn't get through that even wearing a corset.

"It's enough for a skinny person," Lou said. "I tried it and I could squeeze through if I took my shirt off. I set the chairs up as though a six-footer were sleeping on them, feet over-hanging about four inches."

"I was sure it would be more, Lou. The step is ten inches wide."

"But the back of the chair slopes out."

"Don't the legs slope out too?"

"Not as much. It could have been another quarter inch, one-half at best, but that's it. You should be happy, Norma. Lots of people could squeeze through that space. I did."

"I know. Betsy Gilman could walk through frontwards; Danilo Hurkos couldn't get his arm in."

"So doesn't that narrow the list of possibles?"

"Sure. Any starving dancer in a slippery leotard. Thanks heaps, Lou. Next time I'll get an engineer who'll give me the answers I want."

The three of us met Burton at Foo Chow's; I don't know why there aren't any great Chinese restaurants on the West

Side. I ordered. Not that Alexander doesn't know Chinese food, but he's a mood-type eater: By him, four hot spicy roast pork dishes is a balanced diet, provided they have different names.

Burton set the tone for the meal, clumsily, but I don't know how else he could have done it. "Alec," he said, "take a Valium now."

Alexander looked up from his hot-and-sour soup. "The news is that bad?"

"Please, Alec, do me a favor and . . ."

He was approaching it the wrong way. I took out my bottle and handed one of the little yellow pills to Alexander. "Take this to please me, darling," I said. There is nothing I can ask he will not do, if it is to please me, provided I don't give him any reason, or evasive explanation. Alexander swallowed the pill, still looking suspiciously at Burton.

"I don't have a copy of the medical examiner's report," Burton said, "but I can tell you everything in it. The murder knife is an ordinary medium-priced paring knife, with a stiff blade."

"A short knife?" Alexander stopped eating.

"There's more," Burton said. "The length is seven and one-eighth inches and the blade, at its widest, is five-eights of an inch wide. The knife was modified."

"What do you mean, modified?" Pearl asked.

"First of all, the knife was ground down at the tip. The police bought another knife of the same kind and compared them."

"No attempt to grind off the name on the blade?" I asked.

"None," Burton answered. "The tip was ground so as to produce a sharp edge on the back of the blade, making the first two inches a two-sided blade. In the process, the knife lost an eighth of an inch from its original length. Then the wood of the handle was removed, leaving only the tang."

"What about the rivets?" Alexander asked.

"Also taken off, leaving a double-edged weapon seven inches long, one-half to five-eighths of an inch wide, and one-sixteenth of an inch thick."

"Well, that disposes of the thrown knife theory," Alexander said, giving me a look. "No way that knife could have been thrown ten feet. Was there any tape around the handle?"

"Bare. And no fingerprints. The handle of the knife had been gripped by the bottom of Boguslav's blouse."

"Perfect," Alexander gloated. "We've got the killer." He looked reproachfully at Burton. "For this you made me take a Valium?"

"What do you mean, 'We've got the killer?' " Pearl asked.

"Obviously the murderer did not go to all this trouble on a whim, or just to confuse me." In his mind, still, the murderer deliberately killed Boguslav in the adjacent box for the sole purpose of humiliating Alexander Magnus Gold. And, just as obviously, I was the killer, since of the eight of us who knew Alexander would be in that box at that time, I was the only one who had reason to humiliate Alexander, because he outshone me at Rumpole-analysis.

"Why go through all that trouble," Alexander continued, "to take the handle off the knife, making it much harder to grip, risking its slipping or twisting out of his hand, unless there was some overriding reason. And that reason has to come out under analysis. Now that I know it's there, I'll find it. The problem has been changed to a puzzle; puzzles I solve."

"And the blouse." Pearl was excited. "The murderer didn't wear gloves because he knew Boguslav would be wearing a blouse. That proves the murderer knew Boguslav well."

"Pearl," said Alexander patiently, "obviously he knew Boguslav well. You think some stranger would go to all this trouble to kill Boguslav just because he never commissioned a ballet from Twyla Tharp?" He turned to Burton. "I remember it was a silk blouse. Was it by any chance a Russian-type blouse?"

"It was a very loose authentic-type Russian peasant blouse; loose sleeves tied at the wrists, and a low collar. There was white embroidery at the collar and wrists. The blouse was made of fine white silk, completely unornamented except for his initials, VB, intertwined, embroidered in white silk thread, and just below that, over his heart, a tiny blue denim elephant was sewn on. He always wore the blouse tucked into a plaited black silk Russian belt, loose, hanging down over his pants, Russian style. But that night he was wearing his blouse tucked into his pants, American style, behind his Sam Houston belt. When he was found dead, the whole front of the blouse was pulled out of his pants, and threads from the blouse were found on the handle of the knife."

"Who knew he was going to wear a blouse that night?" I asked.

"Everyone," Burton said. "He wore only that one costume as long as anyone knows. But I have more to tell you."

"So who's stopping you?" I asked.

"You are, all of you. Every time I try to describe something, I get so many questions, I get sidetracked. There's another clue. In the hole of the knife's handle, where the end rivet was, there was a piece of nylon monofilament fishing line, tied in a loop. Stretched out, it would be five inches long."

"Or it could go around an object about one and a-half inches in diameter," Alexander said. "What kind of knot?"

"A perfect square knot, with the loose ends cut off very short. The nylon had been melted with a match to keep the knot from slipping open."

"That leaves out dancers," I quipped. "No dancer is smart enough to think of that."

"That's just a myth," Pearl said. "The dancers I know are all very smart."

"A loop is used to hang things," Alexander said. "Were there any nails or tacks anywhere in the box or in the cloak area? Especially in the wooden framework for the new curtain?"

"No nails or tacks anywhere. There were several small nail holes in the wood framework, all at the top corner near the wall. If the knife hung there, the killer could easily have taken the nail out, put it in his pocket, and thrown it away later."

"That would be the perfect place to hide the knife," I said, "in the folds of the curtain. You could find it in the dark in one second. Now I know why the knife had no handle; so it would slip between the layers of the curtain and no one could see it."

"The police thought of that too," Burton said. "None of the threads of the curtain was cut, but the stitches were so far apart—practically basted, it was made in a hurry—that there was plenty of room for the knife to be slipped in between the layers."

"There's another possibility why the knife had no handle," I said. "To slip it into a boot, along the side of the calf. And that explains the loop of nylon. You could put the knife into the boot all the way and just leave the loop hanging to pull out the knife by. No one would notice."

Alexander looked thoughtful. "There's another way to use the nylon loop to hang the knife," he said. "Anyone got some string?" Pearl had a rubber band in her bag. "Good enough," Alexander said. "Now give me one of your chains, Norma, and your wedding band."

I handed him a chain from around my neck and said, "I

never take off my wedding ring, Alexander, and you better not either."

"Okay," he said, "I'll take Burton's." Alexander opened the clasp, threaded the ring on the chain, and closed the clasp. He placed the chain with the pendant ring around his neck. Making a slip-knot in the rubber band, he looped it around the handle of a fork. "Make believe this is the murder knife with the nylon loop," he said. "Now watch this." He pushed the free loop of the rubber band through the ring and then slipped the loop over and around the ring. The fork hung down on his chest. "Under my shirt, the knife would be invisible and both my hands are free, yet I can get the knife off in one second." He slipped the loop back around the ring, and the fork was free.

"Are you saying the killer was a woman?" I asked.

"Plenty of men wear chains these days," Pearl said. "With all sorts of medallions on them."

"You're right, Pearl," Alexander said. "And it doesn't have to be something with a hole in it. With a couple of twists you can hang the knife from a cross, or anything with two or more projections."

"That's a big help," I said. "You've narrowed the list of suspects to a mere hundred million Americans."

"Why couldn't the killer have put the chain right through the nylon loop," Pearl asked, "and yanked it off when he needed it?"

I could answer that one. "Nylon is strong and gold is not. The killer might have torn the chain instead of the nylon and left a clue on the floor of the box which he couldn't find in the dark. Also, if both the chain and the nylon didn't tear, he could have cut his hand on the sharp knife. Alexander's demonstration is not bad, but I like the knife-in-the-boot idea better."

Alexander turned to Burton. "Any more surprises?"

"Plenty. The path of the knife. It went in just under the tip of the breastbone at an angle of forty-five degrees to the midline of the body, right into the heart. It was also angled about forty-five degrees from the plane of the front of the chest."

"No wonder you wanted me to take Valium," Alexander said. "I take it Jeffrey is right-handed?" Burton nodded. "So when Jeffrey said he looked over Boguslav's right shoulder and saw the blood, if he had a knife in his right hand, blade up, the natural motion would describe that exact path." Burton nodded again, ruefully. "That's when the police decided to arrest him?"

Burton shook his head. "There's more. The knife wasn't just thrust in, it was jerked back and forth sideways. With two sharp edges on the knife, the whole anterior portion of the left and right ventricles were slashed, literally, to ribbons. And to end it, the knife was pushed in all the way, to make sure."

"Somebody hated him, all right," I said.

"And to cap it all," Alexander said, "the police found out that Jeffrey hated Boguslav, right? I'm glad I took that Valium."

"We don't know if Jeffrey hated him any more than anyone else did," Burton said. "What the police found out was that Boguslav had been riding Jeffrey, humiliating him with practical jokes in front of the company. And making serious passes at him."

"I thought that when Alexander accused Jeffrey of killing his homosexual lover," I said, "he was just trying to provoke a reaction. So Boguslav was really gay?"

"At least that," Burton said. "The police are checking."

"Does this mean that the killer was right handed?" I asked Alexander.

He thought for a moment. "It could have been done by a

left-handed person, but it would be a highly unnatural motion. Even if the killer were standing on Boguslav's left, it would require that he twist his arm in an uncomfortable way."

I stood up and tried the motion on Burton, on my left. He leaned back in his chair obligingly. It required me to stab upward, with my wrist twisted outward, in a pulling motion. "Very clumsy," I said, sitting down. "Now let's hope that all the suspects but one are left handed." We should be so lucky.

Alexander looked as if he were trying to remember something. After a while, he shook his head in apparent frustration and said, "Why do I . . . ? Something about the knife; something I read once . . . but I can't remember. . . ." He frowned and addressed me. "When is the report on Boguslav going to be ready? Why do I have to learn things at this late stage in dribs and drabs?"

"It's not even twenty-four hours, Alexander; things have been happening so fast that you lose track of time. Pearl is about ready and as soon as we get home I'll go over the Boguslav report and finalize it. You can read it tonight at bedtime."

"I want to talk to that little twerp first thing tomorrow morning, Pearl," Alexander said. "In my office. Tell him if he holds out anything on me, I will kill him personally. And if he's stupid enough to lie, I'll turn him over to Norma."

"We have one piece of good luck," Burton said. "The officer in charge is Lieutenant David Warshafsky."

"That's all I need," Alexander groaned. "He hates me."

"He admires you, Alex," Pearl said, "and respects you. You solved the Talbott case for him."

"That's why he hates me. It's a Gold's Law: Whenever you help someone, he ends up hating you. Well, I've had enough for tonight. Pay the check, Burton, and put it on Baron's bill. Consultation."

"In a minute, Alec," Burton said. "There's just one more thing. To the medical examiner, the casts on Boguslav's knees looked wrong, amateurish. So he cut them off and checked the kneecaps: not broken. Boguslav's arms and legs looked odd, so he took tissue samples: muscle, nerve, bone, and had a pathologist look at them. When he got the results he called Boguslav's personal physician, and it was confirmed. His doctor had never treated Boguslav for broken kneecaps; didn't even know Boguslav wore casts. The reason Boguslav was in a wheelchair was that he was in the final stages of amyotrophic lateral sclerosis."

"Lou Gehrig's disease," Alexander said, turning red. "And the little bastard never told me?" His jaw muscles were clenched, trying to avoid yelling. He breathed slowly, deeply, trying to control it, but you can't control it; even trying makes it worse. It's better to relax, but if you *try* to relax, you make it worse. It was too late. His face turned pale and sweat popped out on his forehead. I jumped up to get to his left-hand pocket in case he couldn't but he got the bottle out first and put one of the tiny white nitro pills under his tongue. Burton and Pearl watched anxiously. Slowly Alexander relaxed visibly. I mopped his forehead with a Wet-Nap, and then his face. Then I mopped my face. Nitro is wonderful stuff, but sooner or later it won't be enough. I had to keep Alexander from getting tense; *he* couldn't. But how?

"Let's go see Jeffrey now," he said. "I want answers."

It was no time to argue with him. I told Pearl to go to the office and finish the Boguslav Report by herself, editing, condensing, everything. I told Burton to go home and leave Pearl alone, that he could not go with us: If I were to kill Jeffrey, and it would be justifiable homicide, I didn't want his lawyer around for a witness. Burton hesitated, but Pearl who, as a woman, has the sense, pulled him along with her.

Alexander didn't want to call first, so we just took a taxi to the Boguslav house. Or, now, Jeffrey's house. When we rang the bell, Pierre Romanoff, in a purple velour dressing gown, answered the door, his straight blond hair falling over his forehead.

12

I couldn't help blurting out, "What are you doing here?"

"You are surprise to see me?" Romanoff said with a heavy French accent. "Then why are you ring the bell?"

"Mr. and Mrs. Alexander Gold," my husband said politely. "We want to see Jeffrey Baron."

Romanoff studied us for a moment, then motioned us in. He pushed a button on the wall of the hall. "Jeffrey will come down right now. Please sit." He led us into the living room.

Jeffrey's voice came down the stairs. "I'm not your servant, Pierre. Don't ring that bell again."

Romanoff rang the bell and called upstairs. "You have the guest, Jeffrey. Please come down the stairs."

"We'd like to talk to Jeffrey privately, Mr. Romanoff," I said. "Is there a place . . . ?"

"The kitchen?" he asked. I nodded.

When Jeffrey came down we went into the kitchen. I moved a chair so Jeffrey would sit opposite Alexander, and then everything hit me at once: The strain of the past twenty-four hours; Alexander's angina attack; the smirking moron sitting in front of me, Jeffrey, who would get one million dollars for failing—for *failing!* I couldn't help it. I grabbed his long hair with both hands and snapped his head back against the chair rail. "You lousy bastard," I yelled, "I'm not going to let you kill my husband." He screamed and tried to arch his back, but I pulled harder. He twisted right so I twisted his head left. "One more lie out of you and I'll rip your scalp off, you understand?"

Pierre slammed through the door, right hand stiff, ready to attack, when he saw me. He stopped and said firmly. "Madame, let him go at once."

"You try anything and my husband will break you in half," I yelled over my shoulder.

He turned to Alexander, who was now standing. "When I have ten years age, I fight the Nazi. You think I have afraid of you? Tell her stop; no torture in my house."

Alexander motioned me to let go. "I apologize for this," he said. "It was fully provoked, but it could have been done differently. We are actually trying to help Jeffrey, I assure you." Alexander moved sideways so he was between me and Romanoff, exposing Jeffrey. "Tell him, Jeffrey. Do you want us to leave? If we do, you can be sure of being convicted of premeditated murder. And the Russian tour will be cancelled. If that's what you want, say so. If not, we will sit down and talk."

Jeffrey shook his head, confused; probably the first time in his life he had to think for himself, without his mother to hold his hand. "Speak, Jeffrey," Romanoff said. "Do you want these people to remain? Or not to remain?" Finally

Jeffrey nodded. Romanoff looked at me. "But there will be no more torture, agree?" Alexander agreed. Pierre left.

"Now, Jeffrey," Alexander said, "tell me about Viktor Boguslav's illness. Everything about it. If I think, just think, that you are leaving something out, or slanting the story, I walk out. And you fry. Is that clear, Jeffrey?"

Jeffrey nodded. "About three months ago, when I moved in here, Mr. Boguslav told me, in confidence, he was very sick, dying, incurable. He would become weaker and weaker physically until he could not take care of himself, or even walk, and within a short time, he would die. I would have to do everything for him, wheel him around when he stopped walking, feed him when he couldn't feed himself, write his letters, everything."

"Why the bandages, the phony story about broken knee-caps?"

"If a man his size fell down the wrong way, on a stair for instance, he *could* break his kneecaps. Then he would have to use a wheelchair. That way, nobody would know he was sick."

"Why couldn't he tell people he was sick?"

"They all hated him. Everybody wanted to be general manager. If they found out, he'd be forced to resign and whoever took over would change everything that Mr. Boguslav had built up. It would not be the Boguslav any more."

"Didn't he own the company personally? How could he be forced out?"

"The company loses millions every year. The Foundation makes up part of it, the board of directors raises the rest. If they really wanted to, they could have made him do anything they wanted."

"But they never did; he had a free hand, didn't he?"

Jeffrey was regaining confidence. "Because he was

smarter than they were, and stronger. If they thought he was weak, they'd tear him apart."

"Why did he introduce a new modern ballet at the Farewell Gala?"

"I don't know." Alexander started to get up. "Don't leave, please, Mr. Gold. I really don't know. He never told me anything."

"Why did you stay, then? I thought you wanted to learn how to run a company."

"I did learn. I watched and I listened. I saw how he worked, how he manipulated people, even rich people, so they'd do anything he wanted. I only didn't know what he was thinking."

"Was there no other reason? Last time you said that when you took over the company . . ."

"He promised me. He said if I took care of him, he would leave the company to me. In his will. He had no relatives at all. And if he lied, my father would stop the Foundation from giving any more money. So there'd be no company unless I was general manager."

"Would the company accept you?"

"They'd have to; I'd make them."

Alexander shifted in his chair wearily. "How long has Pierre Romanoff been living here?"

"Why, all the time." Jeffrey looked puzzled. "He and Mr. Boguslav have lived together ever since they met. Everybody knows that."

"I don't," Alexander said. "So Viktor Boguslav was a homosexual."

"Yes, but . . ." Jeffrey didn't know how to proceed. "He was sort of interested—in all kinds of—experimentation."

"Did he ever try with Susan?"

"That was just flirting; he used to kiss everybody."

"And Roberta?"

"Sort of joking. He said she was the only woman he ever met who was big enough for him."

"And you, Jeffrey. Did he ever flirt with you?"

"I'm not like that."

"Answer the question, Jeffrey." Alexander was clearly losing patience.

"He tried all the time, Mr. Gold. He said I was very attractive. He . . . he . . . he was always touching me. I had to be near him all the time. He even did it in front of people to make it look like . . . And then he would laugh. But I wasn't. I didn't."

"He liked to humiliate you?"

"Not just me; everybody. It was the jokes I hated. They weren't really jokes; he was very cruel at times. Like the time he sent me into the girl's dressing room to get a cabriole. There really is such a thing, you know, I looked it up later, it's the leg of a table. But in ballet, it's like a leap. The girls all laughed at me; they think I'm ignorant."

"Didn't Pierre mind Boguslav's attentions to you?"

"Pierre was used to it, after twenty years."

"So Boguslav mistreated you, worked you night and day, humiliated you, tried to seduce you, fooled you, and you knew it otherwise you wouldn't be thinking about cutting off Foundation funds, and to top it all, he made you pay for the privilege. Tell me, Jeffrey, didn't you hate him a little?"

Jeffrey didn't look like a silly boy any longer. "I was waiting for him to die. Every day I waited. Whatever he did to me, I knew he would die soon and I would win."

"So you waited. Until you couldn't wait any more? And stabbed him?"

"I was asleep."

"Through all that noise? No one believes that, Jeffrey. No one could have gotten into that box without your help. Who was it Jeffrey?"

"They did, whoever did it. I don't know how, but they did. I waited this long, I could have waited another few weeks for him to die."

"But if suddenly you had a reason, Jeffrey? If Boguslav told you something, showed you something, did something, or you found out something, something that triggered you —that made it necessary for you to kill him right then and there . . . ?"

"It's a lie. He lied. My mother never . . ." He stood up and began hitting Alexander with the sides of his fists, like a girl. "Pierre—Pierre—" he screamed. "Get them out of here!" Alexander stood up sadly and walked toward the door. I followed.

Jeffrey collapsed on the table, sobbing. Pierre was comforting him. We let ourselves out.

"Just what I needed," Alexander said. "A motive. Ten motives. Progressive parenting. Shit." He thought for a minute, then said, admiringly, "Can you imagine a guy that size threatening me? Takes guts."

"These ballet dancers, Alexander, they're very strong."

"Yeah. Even so, I must weigh twice as much as he does."

I got a cab. Alexander looked worn out. "When we get home," he said, "call Baron. Tell him I want to interview the five of them, to arrange it, at the theater. And to make them cooperate, talk freely, or else. I don't have time to check things out, to catch them in lies. Three in the morning; two in the afternoon."

"Yes, dear. Which five?"

"The ones Jeffrey mentioned in our first interview with him, when he told us about all the antagonisms in the company. The ones who were unhappy with Boguslav: Spenser, the conductor; the ballet master, Zoris; the two ballerinas, Betsy and Tatiana. And Kurt Tindall. Make that six; add Pierre Romanoff. He has to know Boguslav better than anyone else. Also, he has to know where all the bodies are buried."

"Okay, darling, but I'm going to make it two in the morning, two in the afternoon, and two in the early evening. You'll need time to analyze what you learn in between. And you'll need time to rest, or else you'll collapse." A session like this one with Jeffrey was more strain than ten four-mile walks.

Pearl had the Boguslav Report ready when we got home. She also had hot strong cocoa and a bathrobe and slippers for Alexander. If I ever start a *ménage à trois,* it's going to be with Pearl.

Alexander and I settled down in bed to read.

Two days to go.

13

REPORT: VIKTOR BOGUSLAV

If you were to ask him, Viktor Boguslav would assume a heavy Russian accent and say he was born in Sebastopol, moved the twenty miles to Moscow when he was one year old, and when he was five and his father deserted his mother, made the five hundred mile trip to Odessa to live with his mother's folks.

Most people left it at that, but a few who knew

geography pointed out that Sevastopol was about a thousand miles from Moscow, Odessa was almost as far, and that Sevastopol was spelled with a *v*. Whereupon Boguslav would offer to bet a thousand dollars, or whatever he thought the sucker would go for—"I learn spik Inglish good, no?"—that in Russian what looked like a lower case *b* was pronounced *vee* and that everything he had said was true and accurate and that he could prove it.

He didn't always get a bet, but when he did, he won. If the sucker made a fuss, he would stand up to his full height of six feet, eight-and-a-half inches—which in his high-heeled Texas cowboy boots made him seven feet tall—and full weight of three hundred fifty pounds, and ask the sucker if he wanted to discuss this gentlemanly wager with Viktor's big brother. He never had to ask twice.

Viktor Boguslav, born Caspar Beaufort Smith, weighed twelve pounds, six ounces at birth, which did not endear him to his father and, friends opined, had some bearing on the problems that led to the situations which culminated in Pappy's desertion.

Moscow is a tiny town about one hundred miles north of Houston. Sebastopol, equally undersized, is twenty miles west of Moscow, and Odessa is a mid-sized city one hundred and fifty miles south of Lubbock.

Caspar Smith was a good student and a devoted reader with a real interest in writing, but because of his size—at twelve, he was already six feet tall—the people he liked avoided him. He did not get along with the jocks because he was too slow and clumsy to play with them and too uninterested in sports to talk to them.

Caspar found his own way of getting even with those who rejected his friendship. One particularly nasty jock once pulled a pair of silk panties out of his bag in a crowded locker room. He swore he didn't know how they got there, but for the rest of his life, he was known as "Silky." The initials embroidered on the panties, though she swore she had no embroidered panties, belonged to a girl who had been particularly cruel in detailing why she wouldn't be seen dead with a big clunk like Caspar, when he asked her to a dance.

There was the neighbor's dog who hated Caspar and tried to bite him every time Caspar walked past. One day, the dog was discovered howling in agony, his nose and mouth stuck full of porcupine needles. Pulling out the barbed spines with pliers almost killed the animal. No one knew how the dog could have bitten a porcupine; there are porcupines in Texas, but not in the middle of a city of eighty thousand. For some reason, the dog never bothered Caspar again.

A sadistic teacher who took pleasure in humiliating his students made the mistake of taking on Caspar. For a whole semester Caspar suffered and said nothing. That summer, when the teacher was driving in the Apache Mountains, his car suddenly dropped dead, miles from civilization. It was determined later that the teacher had panicked, left the car, and died of exposure. The car was towed back to the little town of Kent, where it was found that someone had poured molasses into the gas tank. No charges were filed, but no one ever crossed Caspar Smith after that, either. Or came close to him.

Caspar's mother died when he was sixteen. In his loneliness he took to writing long epic poems about the Old West, which featured tall silent heroes who wiped out the evil outlaws and saved the timid townspeople in spite of their unappreciative clannishness.

Caspar not only studied the literature of the Old West, he talked for hours with his grandfather, who had actually lived through some of the times Caspar had read about and who was more of a father to the young man than Caspar's own father had been. Grandfather had a good memory and could repeat perfectly the stories told him by *his* grandfather, who had been a cowboy.

Caspar's poems won the approval of his teachers and were read aloud at the monthly meetings of the Ector County Golden West Historical Society. On the day Caspar turned seventeen, his grandfather, full of joy and pride, gave his only grandson a complete Old West outfit: a ten-gallon Stetson with a real eagle feather in the snakeskin band, a plaid cowboy shirt with button-down pockets; a red bandanna neckerchief clasped in a genuine silver ring set with real turquoise imported from Jal, just across the border in New Mexico; a pair of genuine Levis with copper rivets; and a pair of authentic hand-tooled black-leather pointed-toe high-heeled cowboy boots made to order for Caspar's huge feet. And to top it all—"Might as well have it now as wait till I pass on," his grandfather said—his most prized possession, which he had inherited from *his* grandfather who had received it from the hallowed hands of Sam Houston hisself: the three-inch-wide carefully oiled black leather belt with its famous longhorn buckle, a four-by-six-inch curved steel plate from which the powerfully carved head of a Texas Longhorn steer protruded a full inch, its sharp pointed horns curling out and back in a wide dangerous sweep. "Takes a man to wear that," his grandfather had told him, and Caspar wore it proudly.

Caspar wore that uniform almost every day, all through high school, and acted as though he did not hear the snickers.

Caspar never expected to be able to go to college, but when he won a literary scholarship to

the University of Texas at Austin, his grandfather promised to cover half his living expenses
if Caspar could get a job and cover the other
half. Caspar joined the Poetry Club, the Bronco
Billy Anderson Wild West Film Society, and Les
Amis de France. He made friends with creative
cultured people, boys and girls, for the first
time in his life, and was just beginning to be
happy, when disaster struck.

Because of the war, there was a shortage of
Texas-size healthy males on the campus, which
made life difficult for the football coach. A
man of action, the coach simply press-ganged
Caspar and seven other giants, giving them the
free democratic choice of accepting the benefits of joining the football squad—cheerlead-
ers, the training table, and spending money—
versus suffering the pains of having scholar-
ships revoked and knees broken. The coach did
not accept the excuse of lack of experience or
desire, opining that if gorillas were allowed
on the field, he would undertake to teach them
football in two weeks.

The eight young men quickly saw the point of
the argument and signed up. The coach, having
four other Smiths on the squad, named Caspar
"Jumbo," in honor of P. T. Barnum's giant elephant.

The coach might have been able to train gorillas; he was somewhat less successful with his
assortment of oversized humanoids.

At that time Colonel W. de Basil's Original
Ballet Russe was making its American tour and
had stopped in Austin for a one-night stand at
the large prestigious University of Texas. The
football coach had a brilliant idea, which had
damn well better work because nothing else had
so far. He would take Jumbo and the other seven
of his new-found clod-hopping, tangle-footed,
lumbering, bumbling, boneheaded incompetents

to the ballet so they could watch and learn that not only was it possible for a person to take two consecutive steps without tripping hisself up, but that you could even, with practice, learn not to knock over your own ball-carrier as you fell, and not to get the idea that being graceful was faggish because it wasn't, as some of these fags were in very good shape and a lot stronger than they looked, and to watch your mouth as some of these strong fags were also French fags who learned *savate* before they could walk and would rip your fat belly open with one kick while you were trying to decide which was your right hand, and after they saw what was what, he was going to hire a ballet teacher to show them how to move right, and they had better learn good and fast or else.

The first ballet on the program was *Les Sylphides,* with George Skibine as the sole male dancer. During the overture, the lovely Chopin *Prelude* that seemed vaguely familiar to him, Caspar felt an odd stirring, expectation, curiosity, wonder. When the curtain rose on the softly lit, blue-white misty forest glade, on the little tableau of innocent girls in their flowing white *tutus* centered on the male dancer in his Byronic velvet jacket, Caspar melted. It was as though the great secret of his life had been revealed; the one he had always known had to be there but could never bring forth clearly. The epiphany, the reason for his being alive, was there on the stage. And when the *Nocturne* began, and the girls floated like dandelion feathers across the stage, Caspar Beaufort Smith, Jumbo, cried in overwhelming happiness for the first time in his life. The *Mazurka* began and one of the principal girls bounced lightly, effortlessly, weightlessly across the stage like a bubble on velvet, and

Caspar, eyes blurred by tears, saw an angel hovering over the earth.

Then Skibine danced alone and Caspar fell in love; not like the love he felt for his dead mother, or even his grandfather; not like the yearning, the warmth he felt for the girls who had spurned him; but the love of the worshipper for his god, the created for his creator, for the unearthly being who had opened his soul: the graceful, the elegant, the romantic, the *beautiful* George Skibine. Caspar could only watch the rest of the ballet peripherally; his eyes focussed on Skibine.

Even at rest Skibine, the perfect *danseur,* dominated the stage, standing beautifully, breathing controlled, not showing the effort of his work. Variation after variation, Caspar's eyes stayed on Skibine, wondering, marvelling, how a human being could move so, could be so beautiful; determined somehow to relive those magic moments again, somehow to come closer to that unbearable shining loveliness, that ecstasy of spirit, to become one with that grace, that splendor, that radiance. Caspar knew he would never love another woman. Or another man.

The ballet ended as it began, with the dancers fixed in the opening tableau, hinting at the cyclic eternal repetition, the never-ending heaven of the misty glade, the blue-white glow, the serene loveliness that Caspar longed to be one with. His fellow athletes applauded embarrassedly; Caspar sat unmoving.

During intermission Caspar went backstage, got in unnoticed, and found his way to George Skibine's dressing room. Skibine, surrounded by fans, officials, and reporters, was good-naturedly answering silly questions and accepting congratulations. Caspar could have made his way forward, could have touched his hero, even shaken hands, but he hung back, afraid to confirm the mortality, to disturb the illusion, feeling clumsy, coarse, gross, inadequate, in the presence of this essence of grace, elegance, and beauty. He stayed until Skibine closed his dressing-room door.

Pas de Quatre was next, the ballet that, one hundred years ago, had brought together in concert the four greatest ballerinas of their time. The four lovely girls wafted across the stage like dreams, singly, in pairs, and together, impossibly floating, with no apparent effort, in their simple beautiful patterns. Caspar was charmed, enchanted, but found himself looking for Skibine to appear. When it was over Caspar remained in his seat, eyes closed, letting his new sensing flow through him; feeling, not trying to order or understand, just feeling.

Giselle, the last ballet on the long program, was a women's ballet, as they all are, really, but it did have George Skibine playing Albrecht, the tragic hero and unwilling source of Giselle's madness and death. In the second act, when Albrecht came to the forest to visit Giselle's grave, when Giselle appeared and Albrecht danced with his dead love, Caspar felt a surge of memory of something that had been in his heart, unfocussed, all the years of his life, heavy, sad, bitter, and sweet. He could not see what it was, but the feeling he recognized clearly.

When the Wilis, the spirits of girls who died before their wedding day, appeared and forced Hilarion, who had caused Giselle's death, to dance with them until he died, exhausted, Caspar again felt the flush of enlightenment cleave through him; the vision of those beautiful, unearthly, pure, unattainable young girls, enticing irresistibly the helpless boy to his death, struck a deep fear in his heart.

And when Albrecht returned, when Myrtha, the beautiful Queen of the Wilis, ruled that Albrecht, too, must die Caspar wanted to jump onto the stage, to destroy the lovely deadly spirits, to save, not Albrecht, but Skibine. In the ultimate evil irony, Giselle had to dance with Albrecht until he died from exhaustion, and, it is certain Caspar *felt,* if he did not understand, the symbolism. Albrecht, trying to escape, was forced back again and again by the vengeful gentle Wilis to rejoin the death dance. He leaped higher and higher until he collapsed on the ground just as dawn came. Albrecht was saved, the Wilis had to return to their graves as Giselle bade farewell to her love and returned to her own grave. Albrecht rose and tried to follow Giselle, but too late, her grave closed as he threw himself on the earth over her.

When the curtain fell, Caspar, covered with sweat, his face wet with tears, stayed after the curtain calls were over, stayed until the theater was empty, stayed until the usher gently touched him.

He went back to his room and woke his roommate, trying to express, to share, to convey, choking, what had happened to him. His roommate told him to shut up and went back to sleep. Caspar decided he would write an epic poem, *the* epic poem, on beauty, ballet, Skibine, love, life, everything. He wrote, as they occurred to him, the words, phrases, snatches, ideas, descriptions, in a list, without order, without form, without deliberation. The words poured out, he did not care; tomorrow he would form them, tonight he must record before it all disappeared.

The next day he cut all classes and worked on the great poem. Nothing. Every time he tried to order the words, to show a pattern, to establish a rhythm, the words died on the page.

He worked all day without eating; by evening he had nothing. Resigned, he typed up his lists exactly as he had recorded them the night before, added a short introductory explanation, titled it "Moving Beauty," and brought it to the editor of *Stirrings,* the official mimeographed publication of the Poetry Club.

The next week when it was published, the Club gave it mixed reviews. The ones who loved it called it "concrete," "disordered," and "revolutionary." The ones who hated it called it "sensual," "bourgeois," and "representational." One particularly vicious rival poet was heard to mutter, loudly enough for others to hear, "lyrical."

Caspar decided not to go to the ballet class with the other seven recruits at the suburban Austin studio of the teacher the coach had selected. Later that day, the ballet teacher informed the coach that she would be unable to teach his seven uncoordinated giants anything, including walking upright without their knuckles touching the ground, that she expected the coach to pay for the damage to her studio, and that she would have her husband horsewhip the next football player who came near her studio.

The next day Caspar went to the dance teacher, convinced her that he was not one of the group that had been there the day before in spite of the outward resemblance, told her that he wanted to become a dancer of the type that would perform *Les Sylphides,* and asked her to please teach him how.

She looked at him with pity and understanding and gently explained to him the iron law of cubes versus squares that would doom his efforts: If a person's height was doubled his strength would be increased by four but his weight would go up by eight; all other things being equal, he would be half as strong in relation to his weight as before. This was why a flea could jump a hundred times its own height, a cat five times, a man once, and an elephant, powerful as it was, could not get all four feet off the ground at the same time. And all things were not equal; with increase in size an elephant must have big legs to support its weight, with large pads on the bottom, while a gazelle has slim legs and tiny pointed hooves. This makes it even more difficult for large animals, or large men, to jump or to be ballet dancers.

When Caspar promised to lose weight, starve if necessary, the teacher told him that he would then be a slimmer elephant. Caspar pressed on, swearing he would study hard, practice all day long. "You will become a more graceful elephant"—the teacher remembered every word of that discussion—"but you can never be a gazelle."

Caspar collapsed into tears and told her the whole story; how he had been torn apart by the first sight of *Les Sylphides,* how he fell in love with George Skibine, how he had to dance, he had to, no matter what, even badly.

The teacher took Caspar's huge hands in her tiny ones and confided how her life, too, had been ruined when she was a little girl who didn't know any better and her mother took her to see Anna Pavlova in *Giselle,* and if Caspar was that all-fired bent on ruining his own life, she just might hang around to see that he didn't cause too much damage.

And so began the great, truly loving friendship between the skinny fierce little childless dancer who knew she was a failure and the poor bewitched motherless little giant who had to be a dancer, even if it killed him.

In return for allowing Caspar to use the studio for practice, and for her coaching, and for permitting him to sleep on the floor on a mat-

tress she snuck out of the house, and for the oc-
casional food she was able to scrounge for him,
Caspar kept the place clean, fixed the plumb-
ing, tended the furnace, kept the books, repaired the costumes, and did not tell *anyone* he
was being taught by the teacher.

In spite of his precautions, he was found out,
and his seven fellow football rookies began
ragging him. One day, after supper, he stood up
at the training table and told the seven that he
did not want them making nasty remarks about his
purely professional relationship with his
dancing teacher, and that if they thought their
coarse remarks were all that funny, he thought
it even funnier that the itching powder he had
put into their jocks made them scratch for
hours, and if any more talk like that went on
they just might find scorpions in their jocks
next time, so let's call it quits.

When they got up to tear him apart, he informed
them that he was sure the seven of them could
beat him up, but if they started they had better
kill him 'cause if he lived he swore to God he
would slit their throats in bed one night and
whatever happened to him afterward, they would
be dead. And not to call him Jumbo any more, either.

They sat down again, muttering about guys who
couldn't take a joke, had no sense of humor, and
who were not regular good old guys. All except
one bully, bigger even than Caspar, who crowded
Caspar, as he retreated, until Caspar was
pinned against the wall. The bully swung his
right at Caspar, who twisted to the left. When
Caspar straightened up and twisted to the
right, one of the sharp horns on his grandfather's Sam Houston belt buckle ripped a rough
gash six inches long and almost an inch deep in
his cormentor's belly.

Everyone agreed it must have been an accident,

but no one ever bothered Caspar again nor called him Jumbo again, nor spoke to him again nor went near him again.

Caspar told the ballet teacher that he was tired of football and there was no sense in going to school anymore because he wasn't learning anything worthwhile when all he wanted was to learn how to dance and he didn't care how big he was he was going to do it and if she wouldn't he would find someone who would and that was that and he had left the football team and he had left the training table and he had left the dorm and he had left the school, all of which would give him more time to practice.

Caspar stayed with the teacher, organizing her books and her studio, and studying and prac-ticing whenever the floor was free. He worked at odd jobs in the area and gave the teacher all his money. He asked her to show him how things should be done, even if he wasn't allowed to do them, and to be allowed to watch the classes. The chil-dren soon got used to seeing him around and even the teenagers and their mothers accepted him.

At the beginning of the next New York ballet season he told the teacher he had to go to Ski-bine. She had saved all the money he had given her, and she gave it to him so he could get to New York and live until he found a job.

Wherever he went after that, he wrote to her every Monday, telling her what he did and thought and felt, often in the most beautiful lyrical language. She saved all his letters and wrote to him monthly, her life being less densely packed than his with event and change, offering advice, criticism, and always sup-port. She often, in later years, asked him to allow her to publish those portions of his lovely letters that were fit for publication, but he always refused. Then suddenly, one week before his murder, Boguslav wrote her, in the last letter she received from him, that he wanted all his letters published, unedited and unexpurgated, as soon as possible after his death. Should no publisher agree to these terms, she was to have the book published by a subsidy publisher, and enclosed a check for forty thousand dollars to finance the venture.

He also said that in his next letter he would describe to her his greatest triumph, a feat for the record books that no one else would ever be able to duplicate.

On her seventy-fifth birthday he arranged a Gala Performance in the teacher's honor in Austin, giving an open invitation to all the greatest dancers who were in America, and all her ex-students, to attend at his expense. George Skibine, whom Boguslav was now ready to meet, was director of the Dallas Ballet, only one hundred and seventy-five miles to the north, but Skibine was ill with what was to be his terminal sickness and could not come.

Even Boguslav was astonished at the number of dancers, some of them world-famed, who had been introduced to ballet in his teacher's beginners' classes. It was the happiest and proudest moment of her life, and of his too. The program Boguslav selected was, of course, *Les Sylphides, Pas de Quatre,* and *Giselle.* During the performance Boguslav kept looking around, only later realizing that he was looking for a very young man who was crying. He didn't see one, but found him at the end of the performance, when he realized he was crying himself.

When the nineteen-year-old Caspar arrived in New York, he headed straight for Colonel W. de Basil's Original Ballet Russe, in which Skibine was the *premier danseur.*

Caspar found a cheap apartment near the theater district and a cheap lawyer to change his

name for business reasons and, really, as a re-
birth, to Viktor Boguslav. He bought a cheap
Russian blouse (actually a maternity gown,
since he could not afford custom tailoring yet)
and wore it outside his pants, Russian style, to
hide his longhorn belt, and tied it in place with
a soft, tasseled rayon rope. He tucked his jeans
into the top of his boots and let them blouse
over like Russian pants. In spite of everything, the first person he spoke to called him
"cowboy."

He took to hanging around the Ballet Russe
gofering and performing minor services, asking
for nothing in return. If one of the dancers com-
plained of a splintery spot, he sanded the
stage; if something heavy had to be moved, he
lent a hand. Offered a tip, he refused with a
smile. Little by little he was accepted as part
of the ballet milieu and, on occasion, when
someone was sick or drunk or just missing, he
fetched a prop, or called a principal, or worked
a light. The union did not resent him; the job-
holder got his paycheck and the job was covered.

Viktor hovered near George Skibine, and whenever possible, watched him in class, in rehearsal, during the creation of a new ballet,
and on stage, but never came close enough to
annoy his hero. If Skibine ever noticed the
young giant who always seemed to be around, he
said nothing about it. Had Viktor ever spoken to
Skibine, it is probable that the dancer would
have responded with his customary graciousness
and courtesy, but *Caspar* never dared.

Once, after a performance, while waiting
across the street from the theater so he could
watch over Skibine going home without being noticed, Viktor overheard two young toughs planning to beat up a fag when the dancers came out of
the stage door. Viktor quietly caught up with
them in a nearby alley and slammed their heads

together, knocking them out. He then deliberately dislocated their hips and placed them on
their backs in the basic first position of ballet with, as he wrote the teacher, proper turn-
out from the hips rather than from the knees. She
wrote him a long impassioned letter imploring
him not to use violence except in self-defense.
He never did again or, at least, never wrote
about it to the teacher.

He drifted, soon and easily, into the world of
homosexuals and did not seem to feel any discom-
fort there. And when he ran out of money and the
ballet was to go on tour, he would go with older
homosexuals who would give him gifts of money
and clothes. Since he never asked for anything,
he explained to the teacher, and never went with
anyone he really disliked, he did not consider
himself a prostitute.

By the beginning of the next season Viktor was
so useful that the company hired him as general
assistant to anyone who needed him. He was assistant bookkeeper, assistant wardrobe mis-
tress, assistant music librarian, assistant
booker, assistant stage manager, assistant
fetcher and carrier and messenger and pinner-
upper and paint retoucher and makeup checker
and scrim patcher and trouble shooter, doing
everything that was asked of him by anyone
cheerfully and efficiently for practically no
money. It was the happiest time of his life.

When George Skibine left de Basil and joined
the Ballet Theater, Viktor followed him; but
when Skibine joined the Army, Viktor couldn't.
He tried to enlist with the wild idea of shield-
ing his idol from harm, but was rejected again
because of his height. Although Skibine was
only slightly older than Boguslav, in Viktor's
eyes Skibine was the revered patriarch who must
be respected and protected at all costs. Professionally, this was accurate; Skibine had

started dancing when he was five, as a child in *Petrouchka,* as a can-can dancer at sixteen at the *bal Tabarin,* as an adagio dancer in Paris, and as a *premier danseur* at the ripe age of twenty.

Viktor left Ballet Theater and worked with a series of small companies in any position that was available, often performing several functions at once. Because of the manpower shortage he was welcomed in every company, often assuming responsibilities far beyond his title and age.

When the war was over, Viktor went searching for Skibine, and discovered him working as an interpreter and secretary to an art dealer. There is an apocryphal story that Viktor Boguslav bearded Sol Hurok in the Russian Tea Room and demanded to know why the most beautiful dancer in the world was wasting away as a common laborer. It is in the records, however, that Hurok persuaded Skibine to return to ballet with the Markova-Dolin troupe. The next year Skibine married the beautiful twenty-year-old Marjorie Tallchief, one of America's great dancers, and joined the Grand Ballet de Marquis du Cuevas. Viktor, of course, followed behind.

Over the next few years Viktor continued his worship at a distance and performed his usual untitled functions in the company, while Skibine choreographed several ballets.

Then an extraordinary thing happened, totally unprecedented, which threw Viktor into a panic. George Skibine became *premier danseur étoile,* the highest possible position for a dancer, and his wife, Marjorie Tallchief, became *première danseuse étoile,* simultaneously, of the Paris Opéra Ballet, one of the world's largest companies.

Viktor did not have enough money to get to Paris, much less live there, yet he could not

bear to be separated from the man who gave his
life meaning. He reverted to his old method,
selling himself, this time to anyone no matter
how bizarre his, her, or their tastes. In one
month, so tireless was he in the pursuit of
money, he put together enough to fly to Paris.

He had never lost his love of French; in the
ballet world, French is the language of dance,
so he had little difficulty establishing himself as a useful person to have around the Paris
Opéra.

There too, at thirty-five, he made friends:
London-born Evan Spenser, a twenty-five-year-
old assistant conductor who had yet to make his
mark; Zoris Ziladiev, the dancer, two years
older than Viktor, whose family were all dancers who had escaped from Russia during the revo-
lution, and who had lived, since the age of
twenty, with the certainty that he was a failure, that he was not good enough to get a lead
role in a ballet; and Pierre Romanoff, the
grandson of nobility and, it was whispered, a
bastard son of the Czar, a dancer of tremendous
skill and talent who had been told outright, at
the age of twenty-one, that he would never get a
classic role because he was only five feet, one
inch tall.

Viktor fell in love at first sight when he saw
Pierre in rehearsal, and moved into Pierre's
pension that day. The four oddly assorted resi-
dents of the little house formed a strongly
bonded group that was destined to stay together
for life.

Again, Viktor Boguslav was happy, and, in ad-
dition, had love and friendship.

When I finished the report I looked at Alexander. He had
fallen asleep over the first few pages, the report open on the
blanket. Poor baby, he'd had a very hard day. I quietly took
away the report, tucked him in and put out the light. After

slipping in next to him I kissed him goodnight and in his sleep he put his arms around me.

That's when I love Alexander the best: when he's asleep and I'm watching over him.

14

Alexander finished reading the report just as he finished the terrific Gruyère-garlic omelette Pearl had made; my recipe, naturally.

"I see she's picked up your style, Norma," he said.

"She's a slow learner," I said, "but she gets there."

"I didn't mean it as a compliment, Norma."

"I did." Pearl began serving the coffee. "Great job, Pearl," I said. "Couldn't have done much better myself."

"You put in very little," Alexander said, "about the last twenty years, Pearl. Why?"

"Oh, come on, Alexander," I said. "She had only one day."

"There was too much information," Pearl said. "There are twenty pounds of clippings on my desk. He really was a publicity hound. I figured you could get the same dope from today's interviews, but if you want me to, I'll make an abstract for tonight."

"Okay, but it's probably too late; I'll have to live without it. Why did you go into such detail in his early years?"

"I felt it was important," she said. "A murder like this, carefully planned, had to involve, spring from, the psychology and the personality of the victim as much as that of the killer. When you understand the victim you will be pointed right at the killer."

"She's right, Alexander," I said. "Boguslav was a most unusual and complex combination of Texas schoolboy, Parisian *bon vivant,* and Russian impresario. When we understand how these characteristics fit together, in what balance, it will be clear, immediately, why he was killed, and then, automatically, we will know who did it. There can be only one very oddly shaped key that can fit this particular lock."

"We don't have the time," Alexander replied, "to psychoanalyze the whole ballet company. And if we did, I am sure that *everyone* we talked to would turn out to be at least a little peculiar, except me and thee, and I haven't been too sure about thee, lately. No, what I have to do is figure out *how* it was done, to solve the puzzle, then I'll have the killer." He turned to Pearl. "Are the interviews all set up?"

"Of course, Alex. I gave Norma the list. First one is Evan Spenser, 10:30 at the ballet school."

"Why so late? I've got six people to talk to and I must get to them before Lieutenant Warshafsky does."

"Are you kidding?" Pearl said. "Warshafsky has already worked them all over at least once; some of them two and three times."

"How do you know that?" he asked.

"He told me when I set up his interview with you for this morning."

"Warshafsky?" Alexander was astonished. "But he's not a suspect."

"No, darling," I patted his hand. "But you are."

It finally sank in. He flushed. I cooled it quickly. "Just

kidding, Alexander. You're only a witness. We both are."

The bell rang. Pearl showed Warshafsky in and put a coffee in front of him, then added a bagel with cream cheese.

He looked grateful. And tired. I'd hate to be married to a cop. "You look pooped," I told him. "Why don't you have your nosh and I'll tell you what we didn't see. If I leave out anything, Alexander will correct me, even if it sends me to the chair." He would too; can't help it.

As Warshafsky ate I told him everything I knew, which was little enough. With his coffee, Warshafsky asked Alexander what he had figured out so far.

"The knife is the only real clue," Alexander said, "but I haven't figured out what it means yet. Evidently the nylon loop was to hang it from something, but what, I don't know. Or why."

Suddenly it hit me. "Why hang from?" I asked. "Why not to pull out from? Like a shoe. A ballet shoe, maybe. Otherwise, why did the knife have to be so short? Even Betsy Gilman's shoe has to be longer than seven inches."

"Oh, Norma," Pearl said. "That's impossible. No ballerina could dance with even a tiny pebble in her shoe. That knife was sharp on both edges."

"That's a good point," Warshafsky said. "The knife could have been hidden in a regular shoe, though, maybe with some tape over it."

"Can't be," Alexander said. "Why should anyone put a knife in his shoe? In his pocket, up his sleeve, any place has to be better than a shoe you have to take off."

"How about hidden in the wheelchair?" I asked. "Or taped to the bottom of the chair?"

"We checked that," Warshafsky said. "There are no nail holes or secret slots in the chair, and no traces of adhesive, although that could have been wiped off."

"Forget about all that," Alexander said. "A killer who

planned this well, he wouldn't let that knife out of his possession. Imagine his embarrassment when he gets to Boguslav, God knows how, ready to kill him and finds the knife has been lost someplace. No, he carried that knife on his person, maybe taped to his forearm. Wipes the remnants of adhesive off with his handkerchief, and zip."

"Then why the loop of nylon?" I asked.

"Looped around his cuff button or something, in case the adhesive loosened. From sweat."

"If he used his handkerchief to wipe the knife, why did he hold the knife in Boguslav's blouse?" Pearl asked. "And why did Boguslav let him pull out his blouse without screaming for help?"

"Maybe he was afraid that threads from his handkerchief could get caught on the knife or Boguslav's clothes. And Boguslav was too weak or too slow to stop him from grabbing his blouse." Alexander addressed Warshafsky. "Any doubt that the killer used Boguslav's blouse to hold the knife?"

"None," Warshafsky said. "The pattern of bloodstains, the threads, everything checked."

"One thing puzzles me," Alexander said. "Our report said that Boguslav practically always wore his blouse loose over his cowboy belt, Russian style, with a Russian type cord around it. Then I was told that Boguslav's blouse was pulled out of his belt. Which belt was that?"

"He was wearing his blouse tucked into his pants, American style, like a shirt. He was not wearing the Russian sash, just the cowboy belt. The whole front of the blouse was pulled out and wrapped around the knife."

"That means he was going to wear those sharp horns exposed at the Gala Party," Pearl said. "Why? Those things were dangerous. And if he was planning to play some stupid trick on a guest, how could he do it from a wheelchair?"

"We asked ourselves the same questions," Warshafsky said. "As for the handkerchief, maybe the killer had no place to carry one, like if *she* were in ballet costume."

"Nonsense," I said. "Any girl could have tucked a hanky into her bra. Or a man, into his jock." Pearl had taught me that. And Susan.

"Maybe he was afraid of identification by his sweat," Alexander said. "Or makeup. Or skin condition."

"If so," Warshafsky said, "he was being super cautious. That kind of evidence is only useful to corroborate good evidence. And we checked with Jeffrey Baron. Boguslav had specifically told him to tuck in his blouse when Jeffrey dressed him for that evening, and refused to tell him why."

"Jeffrey dressed him?" Alexander said. "He was that weak and close to death? I take it Jeffrey cleverly didn't volunteer this information."

"Three interviews," Warshafsky said, "would you believe it? I'm absolutely convinced he is too stupid to have done the murder, but no jury would believe that. Mrs. Hanslik," he spoke to Pearl, "please tell your husband to tell Jeffrey, to *order* Jeffrey, to tell me everything. If he's innocent it will help me get him off quicker. And if he's guilty, I'll find out the truth anyway."

"I'll tell him," said Pearl, "but I don't guarantee he'll listen. But I've been thinking, Lieutenant. What about suicide?"

"Suicide?" Warshafsky looked unbelieving.

"He was always playing nasty jokes," Pearl said, "the kind that hurt people. By killing himself in this way, he got everyone he knew in trouble, especially Jeffrey, and ruined the Russian tour, and possibly destroyed the ballet company. *Après moi le déluge*, that kind of thing. And that was what he meant in his last letter to the teacher when he said he would perform a feat that no one else would be able to duplicate. It's perfect."

"And just how did he accomplish this?" Alexander asked softly. Pearl should have kept her mouth shut; Alexander never spoke softly except as a warning.

"Everything fits," Pearl said. "If Boguslav stabbed himself with his right hand, with the blade up, that would account for the odd angle of the knife. He was right-handed, wasn't he, Lieutenant?"

"He was," Lieutenant Warshafsky said.

"And the loop of nylon was so he could pull the knife out of his boot without leaving fingerprints. First he pulled the blouse out of his belt and put his right hand under the cloth. Then, with his left hand, he put the knife on the blouse, gripped the knife with his right hand, and stabbed himself. It all fits."

"It doesn't fit at all," Alexander said angrily. "If he was going to use the blouse to hold the knife with, why have it tucked in at all? Russian blouses are very long. If Boguslav had difficulty dressing himself, might he not have had difficulty pulling out a long blouse? Wouldn't it have been easier to leave the blouse hanging out as it normally was? And I can believe someone killing himself by stabbing, even Boguslav. But to stab himself, and then slash the knife back and forth slicing his heart to ribbons? Even a healthy man might not be able to do that, shock and loss of blood pressure and pain; Boguslav certainly couldn't. And after all that, to be able to push the knife all the way in? Ridiculous."

Alexander would have gone on and on, in his usual over-kill manner, if Warshafsky hadn't interrupted. "Have you come up with anything, Mr. Gold?"

"I don't have the faintest idea how it was done," Alexander said. "I have to talk to some people today before I have enough to even start analyzing the puzzle. Do you have anything I don't?"

Warshafsky hesitated, then spoke. "You'll get it from your spies anyway, so . . . The contents of Boguslav's pockets: a handkerchief, a pocket comb, a nail file, a wallet, an address book, a credit card folder, almost three hundred dollars, and a checkbook. That's it."

Alexander got excited. "No pen? Pencil? Notebook? Flashlight? Nothing?"

"Not even one of those luminous sheets," Warshafsky said.

"Didn't Jeffrey think anything was wrong?" Alexander asked. "First, Boguslav makes him write letters for him. Then Jeffrey has to put up a curtain next to Baron's box because he wants to take notes. Jeffrey dresses Boguslav and there's nothing to take notes with and this dumbbell doesn't notice? Unbelievable!"

"Alex," Pearl protested, "the poor boy was very tired."

Alexander gave her a disgusted look, then said to the lieutenant, "I'd like to talk to you tomorrow morning, after I've finished digesting today's interviews. You may have more information and I may have some ideas. How about Sunday brunch on Columbus Avenue?"

Warshafsky looked a bit embarrassed. "I'm sorry, but I think I have a date for Sunday morning."

"All right," said Alexander magnanimously, "Sunday afternoon."

"Sunday afternoon I visit my kids. It's my only day."

"But my deadline is Sunday midnight." Alexander was really upset. "You may get something I must have to complete the pattern."

"Mr. Gold," Warshafsky said wearily, "I have a whole life outside the police department. If I don't get some rest, some change, I won't be able to function at all. And *I* don't have a Sunday midnight deadline; you do. If I close this case a week later, I still get a gold star." He looked at Alexander's fallen face, and softened. "Look, Mr. Gold, the department is not a one-man show; it's an organization. I have some very good men on my team; you can work with one of them on Sunday. Or else I can meet you here at 5:30. Which is better for you?"

"Neither," said Alexander, "but I can't trust a stranger to level with me. I'll wait for you here. But if you hear anything, please call me. Pearl will be in the office all day and she'll always know where to find me."

"Okay, Mr. Gold." Warshafsky got up to leave. "And if you think of anything, call my office and leave a message. And for God's sake, don't let anything slip about the clothes or the contents of his pockets. I'm taking a hell of a chance telling you all this."

"Don't worry," Alexander said. "I won't. Who knows about the sickness?"

"Jeffrey and Pierre, and the doctor. Don't discuss that either."

After Warshafsky left, Alexander asked Pearl for the reports on the people he was going to talk to. Pearl explained that she had spent all day putting the Boguslav Report together, and all she had on the others was folders full of notes and clippings.

It was almost time to meet Evan Spenser at the ballet school. We picked up the folders at the office so Alexander could skim them in the taxi.

In spite of the driver's wish, I had a feeling we were not going to have a nice day.

15

Evan Spenser, slim, British, and handsome, was checking scores and parts for the Russian tour with an attractive young woman he introduced, before waving her away, as his harpist and librarian. Even for this routine work, he was dressed in a jacket and tie, looking more like a London executive than a performing artist. He insisted on serving tea as we talked.

"I didn't resent Juspada's conducting *Graven Image*," he said. "After all, it was his piece, and he did a good job."

"Did you resent Boguslav's *choice* of a modern ballet with modern music?" Alexander asked.

"Of course I did," he said, calmly stroking his thin moustache, "we all did. We founded the Boguslav as a repertory company for old favorites. And, if we were to do a new production, I should have composed or arranged the music and Zoris done the choreography."

"Who is the 'we' who resented the choice? You, Zoris, and Pierre?"

"Yes, the founders. Tatiana too, since she was with us from the start."

"But didn't Boguslav own the company? Couldn't he do what he wanted?"

"We all provided the first money and the blood, sweat, and tears, so if anyone owned the company, we all did."

"I thought you were all poor in Paris," I said.

"By this time I was assistant conductor at the Paris Opéra, and also arranged music for the new ballets. Zoris was a *régisseur*, had almost stopped performing, just demi-caractère roles and nondancing parts. Pierre was still fighting for recognition, but he worked steadily. Only Viktor had no regular job; just hung around the Opéra and Skibine, doing what he could."

"Then how were you able to form a ballet company?"

"It happened when Viktor got furious with George Skibine," Spenser said.

"I thought he worshipped Skibine?"

"He did, but Skibine went back to America to become director of the Harkness. Viktor felt that Skibine had abandoned him, just as Viktor's father, mother, and grandfather had done. For the first time in his life, at the age of forty-one, Viktor started thinking as well as feeling."

"That was when he founded the Boguslav Ballet Russe?"

"We founded. He told us we would create a ballet company. I would be music director, conductor, arranger, and play the piano in class. And, presumably, sweep the floor. Zoris would be ballet master and *régisseur*. Pierre would be the star dancer, and Viktor would do everything else. We would perform only Viktor's favorites, the *ballets blancs,* the romantic old white ballets, which were in the public domain. White *tutus* would serve the girls for all ballets, and they had better keep them clean. The company would be small, mostly young dancers, who would work cheap. There would be many *pas de deux,* which required no scenery."

"Even knowing you succeeded, it still sounds very improbable to me," I said.

"There had to be an audience tired of weird experiments, discordant music, and ugly movement, which would pay to see the old, beloved, *true* ballets. So we all chipped in. Viktor took every franc we had; we didn't eat that night, but we were happy."

"What you had couldn't have been enough," I said.

"It was the seed money Viktor needed to raise the real money. First were the new clothes for Viktor. He had to be flamboyant, to look like the public's fantasy of a real impresario and to entertain, and even pay off, the newspaper people who would make him a household word. Here was born the wide-brimmed high-crowned Trilby; the full-length black velvet cloak lined with red satin; the five-foot-long ebony staff; the white silk Russian blouse hung loosely over the pants to hide his cowboy belt, tied by a black pure-silk plaited sash-rope with long tasseled ends; the deep purple double-breasted satin vest with the massive gold watch chain across the front; the long black hair combed straight back; and the Mephistophelian Vandyke beard under the huge pointed moustache, which completed the portrait of the eccentric, egotistical, overwhelming, gigantic genius the world has come to know and love."

"So he was acting all the time?"

"He came to grow into the role, and it worked. We gave our first performance only five months later. It was a great success. Then Viktor arranged a European tour and even he was astonished at the size of the audience for his classical ballets. A South American tour followed, which was even more successful, and at last Viktor felt secure enough to arrange an American tour. It started in San Francisco and ended with two full weeks in New York, with a one-night-stand in Austin, Texas, for sentimental reasons. The New York press gave us rave reviews and the audiences went wild. Pierre and Tatiana were recognized as world-class dancers, I as a great conductor, and Zoris as a great ballet master. Viktor was the most interesting personality to hit New York since Salvador Dali."

"I remember the time. Everyone loved the Boguslav."

"The money came pouring in. I hired an assistant conductor, a rehearsal pianist, and a music librarian, though I still did all the arranging and much of the conducting. Zoris picked up some old friends to rehearse the *corps de ballet* and hired more dancers. With the increased budget, he was able to mount bigger-cast ballets with nonwhite costumes: *Coppelia, Petrouchka, Sleeping Beauty,* enlarging the potential audience and giving the dancers greater variety and opportunity."

"So you were established and famous," I said. "Were you all satisfied, happy?"

"Sometimes. But Viktor was very high-handed at times. Ran the company as though it were his personal toy."

"Does that mean you hated him?"

"To know him was to hate him," Spenser smiled. "But you didn't ask the next question, Mr. Gold, to which the answer is yes, I loved him too."

"Does that mean that you're a—, uh—, too?"

"No, it does not mean that I'm an 'uh.' And Viktor wasn't a homosexual either."

"Maybe he never made a pass at you, Mr. Spenser, but he himself admitted . . ."

"Oh, I didn't mean his heart was pure, I meant he should properly best be described as a—, a pansexual. Men, women and children, dogs and cats, hollow trees and flue pipes, you name it. It's been said, and I quote, 'Viktor would screw a rattlesnake if it were dead.' Or alive, whichever is worse, I forget. And he did proposition me, along with everyone he met, regularly, right up to about three months ago."

"When he broke his knees, you mean?"

Spenser looked at Alexander wryly. "Do you really believe that, Mr. Gold? Because if you do . . ."

"Believe what?" Alexander asked.

"Nobody breaks both kneecaps, Mr. Gold. If it were both knees sideways, I would say Viktor was fooling around with some Mafioso's girlfriend. Both kneecaps? That's more subtle. One gunman holding a gun in your mouth, the other—two little taps with a hammer . . . My guess was Max Baron."

"Why would Max Baron do that?"

"Zoris thought it was Baron's wife, but it couldn't be. The way Baron acts about her, he would have fed Viktor his own liver. Fried. I am sure it was because Viktor seduced Jeffrey."

"Why did Zoris think it was Mrs. Baron?"

"Zoris is a dancer; one percent rational, ninety-nine percent emotional, and very romantic. Viktor, even when he was turned down, would always act as though he had a burning hot affair going. Zoris is used to reading surface emotion, just as it is in a ballet."

"And it wasn't so?" Alexander asked. "With Mrs. Baron, I mean?"

"I would bet my life on it," Spenser said. "Viktor couldn't resist a challenge, an opportunity to fool people in a particularly complex plot. He did it to control things, people, to hurt them and twist the knife. He would think it funny while having an affair with Jeffrey, to make Jeffrey believe his mother was having an affair with him, and acting, all the while as though he were playing around with Susan and Roberta, using Max Baron's foundation's money to finance the whole merry-go-round."

"Why would Jeffrey stay with Boguslav under these conditions?"

"Before the beginning of each season Viktor Boguslav

would take on a personal assistant who had to become his slave/lover/gofer/student/son, to be treated with love/hate and to be the repository into which Boguslav sank all his angers and fears and frustrations and hopes. These young men usually lasted only one season. Those who stayed in ballet often attained positions of importance, the idea being if you lived through a year of Boguslav, you could take anything and you had learned everything."

"Was Boguslav really having an affair with the whole Baron family?"

"Oh, he was having it off with Jeffrey all right; he always did with his personal assistants. And probably the younger daughter too, but that's all. Unfortunately, Max Baron believed it all and gave Viktor a subtle reminder that you don't mess with billionaires."

"Do you think Baron killed Boguslav?"

"Billionaires don't make mysteries and implicate their own sons. Their enemies just disappear."

"Who do you think did it, Mr. Spenser?"

"Jeffrey. He really hated Viktor, you know. He was tired, fed up, worried about his mother and sisters, and about how his father would feel, so, when the opportunity arose, he took it."

"Why not a better time and place, when it was less obvious who had done it?"

"A killer is not always rational, Mr. Gold. Or smart."

"Do you really think Jeffrey Baron carried a knife around with him and waited for the chance to kill Viktor Boguslav at a time and place where he would be the prime suspect?"

"It does sound rather foolish, Mr. Gold, but if not Jeffrey, who?"

"Where were you," Alexander asked, "when Viktor Boguslav was killed?"

"Standing in the back of the theater, watching the ballet."

"Anyone see you?"

"I'm sure many did, but none came forward to say so. I've been over this with the police, you know."

"Couldn't you have walked upstairs and slipped into the box, Mr. Spenser?"

"Of course I could, Mr. Gold; I know the theater quite well. But I didn't."

"Who will be the new director of the company, Mr. Spenser?"

"In the past, if Viktor were indisposed for a few days, I would fill in. And he always told me I would succeed him. But my guess is that they'll pick someone from a regional company to handle the business end, and give Zoris the title of artistic director. That way, the company will retain its character and the board won't have to fight with a Viktor Boguslav all the time."

Alexander stood up; evidently there was nothing more to learn from Evan Spenser. I said, "Will you stand with your back against the wall, Mr. Spenser? I want to measure you."

He looked puzzled, but stepped back. The ruler said ten and a half inches chest depth with clothes on. A bit tight, but not impossible. Without clothes? Not likely; but maybe in a thin jersey? And a jacket—the inside breast pocket was a perfect place to carry a small knife. With the nylon cord looped over something hooked into the jacket's lining. Like a safety pin. To keep the knife from cutting the pocket. And Spenser was right handed; I had seen him conduct.

I wasn't counting Spenser out yet.

16

Betsy Gilman was a living doll in her little blue sailor suit. Put a balloon in her hand and she could pass for my granddaughter. Stick a heart-shaped cherry lollipop in her mouth—instant Lolita.

"Make it quick," she said. "I'm cutting the Sunday class, it's a waste of time when you're all hung over—so I don't want to be late for today's. Zoris gets very sarcastic when I'm late." She lit a cigarette, right handed.

Alexander has very firm views about professionalism, so I had to be the bad guy. "Wouldn't it be better," I said, "to go to bed earlier on Saturday night?"

"Oh, I go to bed *very* early on Saturday, and I stay in bed all day Sunday."

"Doesn't that affect your dancing?"

"Absolutely. With Monday off, I'm so relaxed for the Tuesday performance that it takes only one joint and I'm *prima ballerina absoluta* of the whole damn world. The absolute best."

"There are some," I said, "who say that you're a good dancer who got a break because you're so short that you make Pierre Romanoff look tall."

"Tatiana is a shrivelled jealous old bag. She's sore because I took Kurt away from her. I take everyone away from her whenever I feel like it. Viktor I got one hour after I met him." Tatiana Kusnitzova, the shrivelled old bag, is eight years younger than I am. I didn't have to measure to know that Little Betsy Bigmouth could squeeze through, or ooze through, the door to the box.

It was time to strike a blow for us "shrivelled old bags."

"Isn't it true," I asked, "that Viktor Boguslav dropped you at a party in a particularly humiliating way? It was in all the papers."

"Viktor," she spat out, "did not drop me. He planned the whole thing to get publicity. He walked past this barfy blond, a real glandular case, and moved, accidently he said, so his longhorn belt ripped her gown off, leaving her completely naked in front of everybody. Then he looked her over and announced that she was the most beautiful woman he had ever seen, wrapped her in his cloak, and told her he was taking her home to make love the whole weekend."

"What makes you say he planned it?" I asked.

"He always wears his blouse over his belt; it's too dangerous. So why did he tuck his blouse into his pants that night, huh? And she didn't have a scratch on her. Not one."

"This was insulting to you, wasn't it, in front of all those people?"

"Oh, I saw what he was doing. And I went home with the handsomest man at the party. And on Monday, Viktor spent the whole day with *me,* and told me how stupid the fat piggy was."

Alexander decided that it was time to get down to business; to me, this little talk *was* business and had given me a hot idea. "Where were you," he asked, "when Viktor Boguslav was murdered?"

"In my dressing room," she said.

"Anyone with you?"

"A married man."

"Would he swear he was with you during *Graven Image?*"

"I'll give you ten married men who will swear I was with them on top of the Empire State Building."

Alexander gave her a doubting look. "Do you mean that you were really alone?"

"I always warm up before a performance," she said, "but don't let it get around. Why deprive the bitches of their gossip?"

"Where do you warm up? In your dressing room?"

"In the hall. My room is too crowded."

"Wearing your full costume?"

"And get it all messed up? Just a sweat suit, leg warmers, and slippers." Legwarmers? Perfect to tuck a knife into.

"How far is your room from the stair next to Boguslav's box?"

She sighed. "The police went through that already. About twenty feet. And I could have snuck up and down in one minute."

"Wasn't there a panic bolt on the door to the Grand Tier level?"

"Nothing works in these old houses. But so what? Can't a woman open any lock with a hairpin and a nail file?"

Alexander changed the subject. "Weren't you angry when Boguslav went back to Pierre in preference to you?"

"Big deal," she sneered. "Another married man going back to his wife. Happens all the time."

"Didn't it bother you, Betsy?"

"Sure it bothered me, you moron." Her eyes filled with tears. "It bothers me all the time, especially when you get dropped for a man. Why don't you ask Pierre if it bothered him? Why don't you ask Tatiana if it bothered her? And why don't you ask Kurt, that lying son of a bitch? Ask him why he can't love anybody; God damn—monosexual."

"Betsy," Alexander asked formally, "did you kill Viktor Boguslav?"

"When I confess," she got up and stalked off, then turned at the door, "I'll do it to Lieutenant Warshafsky. He's much better looking than you are."

I took Alexander to a health food bar near the school. Over an insipid lentil soup—I guess real olive oil is too expensive—I told him my idea.

"Visualize this," I said. "Betsy puts on street clothes, so if anyone sees her she wouldn't look out of place on the Grand Tier level. No makeup; it's very hard to recognize a dancer you've only seen on stage; ballet makeup is very exaggerated, and if she were seen, no one would know who she was, especially if she wore high heels and slacks. She goes up to the Grand Tier by the fire stair—the ushers are loafing near the main stairs, or if they're ballet students, are watching the new ballet.

"When she tries to open the door of the box, Jeffrey's chairs are in the way. She slides in and tells Jeffrey she just wants to see Viktor for a minute. Before he can say anything, she goes through the curtain, takes the knife from her bag, leans over Boguslav's right shoulder and slips the knife in, just the way you said Jeffrey could have done it.

"She goes back to the cloak area, puts her arms around him with his head pressed to her bazooms so he can't scream, and tells him: a) that she's just killed Boguslav, b) he can scream later when the ballet is over, and c) if he tells, she will confess and say that it was all Jeffrey's idea, he made her do it, and since she's prettier than Jeffrey, and has just turned state's evidence, she'll get off with weekly home visits by a handsome probation officer while Jeffrey gets twenty-five in the slammer, so Jeffrey better keep his big mouth shut.

"She then removes her bazooms from Jeffrey's face,

gives him a big sexy kiss, tells him that if he's a good boy there's more where that came from, congratulates him as the first to know he's going to be the new general manager of the Boguslav Ballet Russe, and wouldn't it be wonderful if the second thing he did was to get rid of the shrivelled old bag and announce that Betsy Gilman is the absolute top ballerina in the universe, gives him another super-sexy kiss and trips lightly down to her dressing room to pick the proper date to inform Lucky Jeffrey that she is going to be Mrs. Billionaire's Son Baron or else, so relax and enjoy."

Alexander stopped eating, a bad sign, and put his head in his hands, a worse sign. "Did it ever occur to you that if Betsy were smart enough to figure out how to kill Boguslav, she might not want her selected future rich husband charged with the crime?"

"Maybe she figured with his money he could plead permanent insanity temporarily? And then, six months later, have a miracle cure? Happens all the time."

"You're dead wrong," he said, "and I can prove it."

"Prove it? How the hell can you prove it?"

"Simple. You're wrong, because if you're right, Jeffrey is accessory before, during, and after the fact, and I have to give Max Baron one hundred thousand dollars."

A logical refutation if I ever heard one; scratch one really terrific solution.

17

Although his hair was gray, Zoris Ziladiev didn't look any older than Alexander. And his step was lighter. He seemed less comfortable sitting in his office chair than he did standing up, although he had just finished giving company class.

"I understand you come from a family of dancers," I said.

"All dancers," he said in a very thick Russian accent. "Father, mother, all grandfather, grandmother. Also wife."

"And your children are carrying on the tradition?"

"Four children. Not dance. Say too much hard work. Crazy." He looked out the window. "Not hard *work;* work *hard.* You like baseball? You work hard; play good. You like footsball? Work hard, break leg. Still be happy. Dance not work; dance pleasure, life. Work; pleasure. Work hard; more pleasure. Not dance is crazy."

I could visualize him looking at the hordes of doctors, lawyers, farmers, taxi drivers, pitying them for not dancing, wasting their lives away not dancing, wondering why, puzzled that they did not just stop their senseless striving and dance, as a real human should. I wasn't sure he was wrong.

"You were one of the founders of the company," I said. "Weren't you taking a big risk at your age, with a family to support?"

"Life can not to be in mud, stuck," he said. "Must to fly, like dance; must to take chance, not be all time safe. Also must to help Pierre. I see could be great. I know. Better as Nijinsky. But not have chance in Paris Opéra. Also Tatiana. Inside she is Markova. I see; Paris Opéra not know yet."

"You discovered Tatiana Kusnitzova?"

"I tell Viktor go get. Tatiana is sixteen, not yet smart. Little girl but big heart. I tell Viktor go to Mama, make promise Tatiana be big star. Boguslav swear he get Tatiana, be nice for Mama, be nice for dog, cat, everybody. He get. Is not beautiful Pierre and Tatiana?"

Alexander was impatient. "I understand you resented Boguslav's interference with your work."

"I throw out. Every day I throw out. Say you come in class, I kill dead."

"Did he believe you?"

"He laugh. Old time, he come sometime. After break knee, every day come, every day I push out."

"Did he resent that?"

"He laugh. Very funny." Ziladiev frowned. "Not funny for laugh. Impresario do money, ballet master do dance. Not can be two ballet master in dance."

"Why did he want to interfere with you? Was he dissatisfied with your work?"

"Me?" Ziladiev looked insulted. "Twenty year I make perfect, now I make bad? No. Boguslav jealous. I know. Not like be impresario; like be *régisseur*. I say not can be, not enough smart. Be impresario? Okay. Be *régisseur*? Must start four year old, learn, work, maybe, maybe."

"Why did you and the others let him produce *Graven Image?*"

"Not let, board of directors let. Boguslav artistic director, general manager; Ziladiev only ballet master."

"Yet you did put it on. Couldn't you have refused?"

"Not refuse, quit. Say I go Baryshnikov, Balanchine, Joffrey, assistant, better as do shit. He say you quit, I break knees, not head, ballet master not can need head, laugh, funny. Also say he love me, please must do *Graven Image*. Beg, please."

"Why did he want to introduce that type of ballet in the repertoire?"

"Why? Not say, but I know. He want be dancer. Not be good role in classic ballet, romantic ballet for giant who not can dance. Must to make new ballet."

"Then why not get Tudor or Balanchine? Why Augustine?"

"Tudor, Balanchine great artist, genius. Do what he want, not what impresario say. Constantine crazy bastard, like Boguslav. Boguslav say principal role must to be giant, not dancer. Constantine think funny joke, okay, he do. I laugh too, funny joke, Boguslav break leg, not can dance, must to get Hurkos last minute."

"I though Hurkos was retained several months ago."

"How long take make new ballet? Five minutes? Lucky Hurkos strong, smart, move good. Work hard, I teach, every day. You see Hurkos on stage? Pretty good work."

"I thought the whole company did well. I particularly liked the jumping line scene."

"That scene okay; rest very sloppy. Must make better. More rehearse. You not see, I see. All crazy Augustine fault. Make movement not from ballet. Why? He dancer one time; know right way. Very hard work, learn crazy movement."

"Well, I enjoyed the dancing very much," Alexander said, "even though the music was harsh."

"Not important," Ziladiev said. "Music nice, help. Happy dance, happy music; sad dance, sad music; okay. But is more important beat. Rhythm. Make dance for any music, but must to follow beat. Is how I teach. *Graven Image* music strong beat. Good."

"So Boguslav made you do something that went against your artistic sensibilities."

"Not make; I pity. Sad. Boguslav no good bastard, but want be dancer. Big, fat, old, not can be dancer. Boguslav bastard, but love dance. So I say okay. I do for him. But next season I be artistic director. He promise."

"And you believed him?"

"Nobody believe impresario. Impresario all time lie, must to lie, can not be impresario and not to lie. But I say Boguslav write letter, like contract. He write, I keep. Next season I make back right all change he make."

"What kind of changes?"

"Plenty. *Petrouchka.* Charlatan not have whip, only have magic flute for make doll come alive. Bear man have whip, for bear only. Boguslav take whip, he say for hit bad dancer. Hah! Hit everybody, even Pierre, even Betsy. I say you like hit, okay, hit Tindall, stupid bastard."

"You were angry with Tindall?"

"Tindall think dance is muscle. Stupid. Dance is heart, soul, beauty. Not how high, how *good.* Could be second Nijinsky, second Romanoff. Maybe better. I teach. No. Tindall like jump. Stupid."

"Why keep him then? Why not fire him?"

"Why? Stupid bastard audience. See jump, applause. See big jump, big applause. Buy more tickets. For beauty, one thousand people pay; for acrobat jumping, one million. You impresario, you fire big jumper? Hah!"

"It seems to me, Mr. Ziladiev, that you disagreed with Boguslav about everything, resented his interfering with your work, hated his changes in the ballet and his lying to make you put on a ballet you hated. Did you hate him enough to kill him?"

"Is enough be impresario, everybody want kill. I want, wife want, Evan want, stupid Jeffrey want, even usher want. Is normal. But I not kill make secret. I kill in class, everybody make happy, much applause."

"So, did you kill Viktor Boguslav?"

"Gold, you not hear? I kill impresario, I tell all people look, I do good thing. But why? You think next impresario better? Hah! Maybe even be impresario who hate ballet, how you like that? Better bastard like Boguslav as different kind bastard."

Alexander seemed to be enjoying Ziladiev as much as I was. "When you took Boguslav up to his box that night, did you notice anything unusual?"

"Always with Boguslav is different. He say put in corner like so, take five minutes make perfect. Big fat bastard."

Evidently remembering what Spenser had said, Alexander asked, "Did you also love Boguslav?"

Ziladiev looked surprised for a moment, then said, "Viktor love ballet more as life. Like me. How can not to love such man. Even if liar bastard impresario, must."

"Where were you, Mr. Ziladiev, during *Graven Image?*"

"In Romanoff dressing room. Put on makeup.

"Makeup? What for?"

"*Petrouchka.* Boguslav not can dance Charlatan, so I must do."

"You know the role?"

"*Régisseur* must to know all roles. In head is more as one hundred ballets. More. All roles, even *corps de ballet.* You think I not know *Petrouchka?* Hah!"

"Did Pierre mind?"

"What for mind? He dance, I make up. When finish *Graven Image,* Pierre do makeup for *Petrouchka,* I go all around check costume, makeup, everybody."

"Anybody see you?"

"How somebody see me in dressing room?"

I had to ask. "Do you wear boots as the Charlatan?"

He looked at me as though I were stupid. "You not see *Petrouchka?* Never?"

"I love *Petrouchka.* But the Charlatan wears a long gown. It's hard to tell if he's wearing boots."

"Charlatan must to wear boot. Is winter, Petrouchka. St. Petersburg. Cold."

That was that. We left.

We didn't talk for a while. With his broken, powerful, rough, poetic language, Ziladiev made me feel the way I did when I watched *Petrouchka* danced by Romanoff. Alexander finally said, thoughtfully, "I have a feeling, a strong feeling, we learned something important, but I can't put my finger on it. Did anything strike you, Norma?"

Alexander asking me? Were we in that bad a shape? "All I learned, Alexander, is that Ziladiev didn't kill Boguslav. Do you feel the same way?"

"Not unless he's a better actor than I think he is. Cross him off the list."

Progress. We now had only five major suspects. Plus Jeffrey.

18

"But certainly," Pierre told Alexander. "Viktor and I make unusual couple. You think you and Madame are not unusual? Everybody is unusual. The true love, it is unusual."

"I agree," said Alexander. "Although most of the people I know are still together, there is an increasing tendency to divorce at the sightest sign of conflict."

"You are referring with delicacy," Pierre sounded sarcastic, "to Viktor's unfaithfulness?"

"It does seem strange that you stood by him in spite of everything. It is well known that you are temperamental, explosive in your work."

"But of course, in the dance, everything must be just so. You think the good performance is with luck? No, it is with attention to every detail to be perfect. In life, one does not control the other person. Viktor, he is how he is; I cannot change him. I am how I am and cannot even make myself to change."

"Didn't it trouble you, his constant chasing?"

"You think I like it? Much was for business; that I understand. Much was for—I do not know what. He had a craziness, you know? Must have everything, eat everything, drink everything, taste, try—like little boy in shop, want this, want that, all."

"Yet he always came back to you?"

"He never leave me, just little visit. I am, for him, first real love; one is never forget first love. Before he know me, even, he love me; when he watch me dance. Then he meet with me, bang, like explosion. For me too."

"And for twenty years he betrayed you and then came back? And you took him back?"

"He must come back and I must take him back. I am his permanence; he is my only one. I, I alone, love him, understand. To understand is to forgive, no? Others, they use him, take from him. I give; he cannot live without me."

"You seem to be living without him," Alexander said quietly. "I was hesitant to disturb you; thought you'd be in mourning."

"My mourning," Pierre said sadly, "it was many years ago. When I finally realize where my love has bring me. Now there is work to do; the Russian tour must be the great success."

"Who will take Viktor's place now?"

"For now, I am. It is logical. Other than Zoris, I am most experience. Also most famous. I have some Russian. And it is funny, Viktor would enjoy, a Romanoff come back to conquer Russia."

"And after the tour?"

"That is up to the board of directors. But Viktor promise to me when he will announce to the board that he is retire, he is not in good health, then he will tell them they must make me general manager and artistic director. They always do what he tell them."

"Did he give this to you in writing?"

He stared at Alexander incredulously. "You give to Madame in writing that you give her the mink coat?"

"No, but I am not an impresario."

"To me," Pierre said, "Viktor is not just impresario. Also, he would not, cannot, hurt the Boguslav Ballet Russe. He is professional, like me. Who else to choose? Zoris? Too old, not interested in business. Can Evan be general manager? Very nice, talk beautiful, but just music, not dance. Stranger? From where? Alaska? Sakhalin? Karachi? No. I am the logical one to be select for permanent position."

Alexander must have had in mind, as I did, Ziladiev's written agreement, he changed the subject so rapidly. "What did you think of *Graven Image?*"

"Not bad," Pierre said. "When first he tell me, I am think maybe Viktor is drunk. Augustine for the Boguslav? Insanity. But Augustine does good job. Professional."

"Will you do any dancing, Pierre, after you take over the company? I mean, nondancing roles, the way Viktor did."

"No. I am too old to dance well; I do not have the *élévation* any more, and I will not go out to dance badly. And after one is a star, it is not fitting to dance only *demi-caractère* role."

"Then Kurt Tindall will be the star?"

Pierre's face flushed dark. "Never!" he shouted. "I will not permit. He is not professional. He will not learn. He is monkey, not dancer. You see him? Always with the stupid smile on the face. Sad dance? Smile. Die? Smile. Go crazy? Smile. You know why? I tell you. He look at the audience, there is not the audience, only the mirror. In his mind is only there the mirror. He see Kurt Tindall in the mirror and say, 'How beautiful is Kurt Tindall. Kurt Tindall is most beautiful object in the whole world.' So happy smile on Kurt Tindall. Only one ballet for him: *Afternoon of a Faun.* Perfect. Not Nijinsky *Faun,* Jerome Robbins *Faun.* Where dancer is in practice room and all the time look in the mirror. Girl come in, beautiful, practice too, could be friend if permit, touch together but he pull away, go back look in the mirror. Perfect for Kurt Tindall."

"I take it, when you become general manager you will fire Kurt Tindall?"

"Immediately. Take anybody else from the street. Could not be worse."

"With you retired and Tindall fired, what will the company do for male leads?"

"There is one nice boy in the company, nineteen, very good, very serious, my understudy. I teach him in private. Tomorrow, yes tomorrow, he could do not too bad. In one year he could be *premier danseur*. He will take my place. Tindall? I get guest artist for one year, develop ten other dancer, twenty, in one year much better than Tindall." Pierre sounded contemptuous, but a bit angry too.

I wanted to get him off Tindall, so I asked, "Who do you think killed Viktor?"

I didn't quite succeed. "Should be Kurt Tindall," Pierre said, "all the time bother Viktor to make him be over me. But Kurt is too stupid. Must be Jeffrey. Who else can do it?"

"Why should Jeffrey want to kill Viktor?" Alexander asked.

"Viktor was one cruel man. Very bad to Jeffrey. Say it is good for Jeffrey, make him learn, but it is lie. Viktor always play joke on people, but on personal assistant always much worse. And on Jeffrey, even more. Maybe because Jeffrey is son of rich man."

"Jeffrey could have left, couldn't he?"

"No, Mr. Gold," Pierre answered. "You do not see. Jeffrey is afraid of father, rich, successful. Jeffrey cannot quit, fail. So he stay until he go crazy, *cafard*, then kill."

"Why then? Why there?" Alexander was insistent. Pierre just shrugged helplessly.

We left. The Eclair was not too far away and we needed

a place to sit and rest, and to call Pearl. Pearl had not heard from Warshafsky at all; nothing else new. Burton was worried. So what else?

Over tea and *Schwarzwalder Kirschtorte,* soul food for that spiritual lift, we relaxed. "How many others," I mused, "did Boguslav promise to make general manager?"

"Everybody," Alexander said. "Wait and see. Even the ushers. You heard what Ziladiev said about impresarios; they have to lie."

"Well, there's a motive: ambition."

"Motives we have no shortage of," he said. "I think if you threw a handful of rice up in the air in here, every grain would hit someone who had a reason to hate Boguslav."

"So good," I said. "Let's find some idiot dancer and frame him. Offer him a hundred grand to confess, we'd still be nine hundred ahead. Make that a million, considering we could have lost a hundred."

Alexander has no sense of humor when he's frustrated.

19

"I would rather say," said Tatiana Kusnitzova with a wry smile, "that Betsy ate my leftovers."

Tatiana looked surprisingly small in street clothes, unlike her stage presence, which radiated power, speed, and strength. She had the slightly horsey look some very tall girls have, incongruous on such a small frame. From a distance she looked like a wealthy New York matron; up close she had the tight drawn look of a marathon runner. Her soft brown hair was still pulled back in a youthful dancer's ponytail. From the neck down she was twenty, but her eyes had seen a thousand years. She was wearing a heavy silver chain around her neck, holding a Star of David. The Star was made of two heavy, hollow silver triangles, one on top of the other. There was a hexagonal hole in the middle that reminded me of Alexander's demonstration with the rubber band. A nylon loop could easily hang a small knife from that Star. When she saw me staring at the chain, she quietly slipped the chain and the Star into her blouse. With her right hand. Wasn't there a single lefty in the company?

Alexander asked mildly, "Would you call Viktor Boguslav a leftover?"

"No I wouldn't." Tatiana looked tired. "He was a great man. But that was twenty years ago. Betsy was still peeing in her diapers then. Her five-minute tupenny-upright, as they used to call it in London, hardly qualifies as stealing someone away. Even Pierre didn't mind her."

"I take it Viktor Boguslav was important to you."

"I was not even seventeen," she said. "And innocent. Really naive. You know what a dancer's life is like? Nine classes a week. I was taking three more with a private coach. Twelve- and thirteen-hour days; grabbing a quick bite between rehearsals. Having to remember forty or fifty ballets; having to look light and beautiful even if your muscles hurt or your feet are bleeding. Always tired; never enough sleep."

She stopped and looked away for a moment. Her voice softened. "It's a wonderful, exciting life, but it's not the way to grow up. It's as closed as a nun's life, surrounded by other girls. The boys, the beautiful boys, are tired too, harried, always being pursued by wealthy homosexuals. And the fear, always the fear. Am I a failure? At seventeen? Will I never get out of the *corps?* What can I do to make someone notice me? Baronova, Toumanova, Riabouchinska, others, were stars at sixteen. I'm almost seventeen; have I lost the race already?"

I couldn't let Alexander say something inappropriate, so I spoke first. "And this is when you met Viktor Boguslav?"

"Like a fairy-tale giant come to save me," she said. "I would be a star; I would dance with Pierre Romanoff. The world at my feet. They would love me; riches; fame. I was so beautiful, how could he resist me? He must love me, he must have me, we would conquer the world together, sign here."

"He proposed to you?" I asked.

"I thought so. A young girl's dreams. He never did, really. He just—let me think. I told my mother and she slapped me. She had divorced my father for me, just for me. So I could go to Paris and become a star. She wanted to go to Paris to be an artist—but it was all for me. Boguslav was screwing her too."

"That's when you left him?"

"No," she said simply. "He left me."

"But you did become a star," I said.

"Oh, yes. Lucky me. Now I take only six classes a week. And my calves knot up only a few times a season. And I can afford massages. And I can even sneak a hot dog once a week and an ice-cream cone once a month. Such sinfulness."

"Your picture is in the papers with a different man every month," I pointed out.

"Different?" She smiled that same tired smile again. "I hadn't noticed."

"You still love him?" I asked.

"I still hate him," she said. "He took away everything I really needed and gave me everything I never wanted."

"You could have left fifteen years ago," Alexander said, "and gone elsewhere. Married, had children, whatever you wanted."

She looked at him coldly. "You could have stopped eating," she said, "fifteen years ago, and been slim by now." She softened. "I couldn't and you couldn't either, Mr. Gold."

Time for me to break in. "Didn't you find it difficult, Miss Kusnitzova, to work with him under these conditions," I asked.

"Not difficult," she replied, "impossible. But he needed me; the company needed me. After our first New York success I advised him to enlarge the board of directors, all millionaires, naturally. He spent more and more of his time on fund-raising and began getting grants from foundations. I took over some of the policy decisions; quietly, of course."

"So you were the one who—?"

"Don't underestimate Viktor," she stopped me. "He was smart and ruthless. I advised him when I saw an opportunity for us. As soon as we had the backing I told him to buy the studio building so we could have a school. This was our base. Then we arranged a long-term contract with the Temple Theater. That, finally, was what fully established us."

So. Again. Ahead of every great man is a greater woman. I could see that Alexander was dying to get on with the questioning I had interrupted. "Why," he asked, "did Boguslav do *Gala Performance* at the Benefit?"

"Well," she said, "it's a good show, funny, and appropriate for a gala where half the people don't really like ballet and half of the rest don't understand what they're looking at. But," again the wry smile, "the real reason was to needle me."

"But you were the star, weren't you?" he asked.

"There are three stars in *Gala,* each one more vain and
nasty than the other two. He brought in Tamara Boruskaya, for her first performance in America. Why? You think
the critics will say one word about me? And that's not van-
ity, that's business. You want to introduce a defector, pick
an evening when you show only her specialties and don't
put any other competition on the stage. He not only puts me
next to her, he brings in Irina Trebshinska, who's almost as
good as I am. Two of the greatest in America, the world, to
be compared with a new, underrehearsed, scared defector?
Now he can offer Tamara half what she's worth. He may
have ruined her career in that one night. That's real bas-
tardly."

"Why would he want to do that?"

"Who knows? Maybe he thought it was funny; he had a
real coarse sense of humor. Maybe she refused him; nobody
is supposed to refuse the impresario. And what about Irina?
Why did he bring her in? I'm sure he didn't pay her; told her
it was for charity, that her presence would ensure a full
house. Bullshit. The house was sold out a month ago, because of Max Baron. The poor kids, the students, couldn't
even get standing room. No, he did it to make me look less
the star."

"What would you have done, Miss Kusnitzova?"

"Put in three of our most promising soloists. Let them
have the fun and the honor and the exposure. Let them be
prima ballerina for one night, they deserve it. Give them
hope, give the whole *corps* the idea that they, any one of
them, can rise within the company. That's the way to
build spirit, the way to get depth and strength in a company."

Alexander looked as though he was flipping a coin men-
tally, then seemed to come to a conclusion. "Is that what you
would do if you were general manager?"

She looked him in the eye and said, "That's what I *will* do *when* I'm general manager and artistic director."

"What makes you think . . ."

"You men," she interrupted, "always think 'male' when someone says general manager. Did you ever hear of Ninette de Valois, Lucia Chase, Marcia Haydée, and dozens of others? You think I couldn't do it?"

"I'm sure you could," he said soothingly. "But what makes you sure you will? Viktor's promise?"

"Promise, shit. Viktor's promise is worth less than shit. In fact, it's a guarantee of nonperformance. I have it as a written contract, and my lawyer wrote every word, that at the beginning of next season, I take over."

"Doesn't the board of directors have something to say about that?"

"They'll do what they're told; they always have."

"Does that mean you'll take over now? For the Russian tour?"

"My lawyer says to wait until the tour is over, in case it goes bad."

"So Viktor's death was a godsend to you?"

"To the whole damn world, it was."

"When did he sign this paper?"

"Two years ago, when I threatened to leave."

"No announcement?"

"That was part of the agreement."

It was enough. I put the next questions to her perfunctorily. "Where were you during *Graven Image?*"

"In the back of the Orchestra, watching."

"Did you see anyone you knew?"

"No. And I was in street clothes; people don't generally recognize artists in street clothes."

"Evan Spenser was in the back of the Orchestra, and he says he didn't see you. Surely he would recognize you."

"And I didn't see him either," she said pointedly. "There could be several explanations for that, Mrs. Gold."

"Did you go up to the Grand Tier?"

"No, what for?"

"To kill Viktor Boguslav?"

"Why would I want to do that?"

"You already told us. Do you want to elaborate?"

"Go to hell," she said, and stalked away.

"Alexander," I said, "complete this couplet: 'Hell hath no fury like a woman scorned.'"

"'No rage in Heaven,'" he recited, "'like love to hatred turned.' But I don't remember the next line, where it says how she got into the box. Do you?"

I didn't. That's the trouble with poetry: lots of feeling, but no substance.

20

Beautiful Kurt Tindall was combing his beautiful golden hair with a beautiful tortoiseshell comb in his beautiful dressing room. Alexander and I spoiled the effect.

"Betsy Gilman is highly disturbed," he said. "I never said I would marry her. Or anyone else. Although I get offers all the time."

I signalled Alexander that I would do all the questioning

lest my dear husband vomit all over the beautiful carpeting. "Was Viktor Boguslav one of your suitors?"

He looked at me unbelievingly, as though it were inconceivable that anyone who met him could fail to fall under the spell. "Of course," he said. "Viktor could hardly keep his big ugly hands off me, even in public. But I don't associate socially with crude people."

"Boguslav is supposed to have impeccable taste and artistic judgment," I said.

"Good taste? My God, have you seen the latest picture in the papers? Viktor in between two elephants standing on their hind legs, all three of them in pink tutus?"

"That was just for publicity; part of his image."

"And midgets," he kept on, "Viktor is crazy about midgets. Really loves them."

This was too much. "You wouldn't say that in front of Pierre," I said. "He'd kill you."

"Pierre," he scoffed. "I'll soon be rid of him." All the time we were talking he was looking at himself in the mirror, adjusting his makeup. Right handed. Occasionally he would see me, but only in the mirror.

"When you're general manager, you mean?" Why not? Everyone else was, potentially.

"They can get some bookkeeper for that," he said. "I'm going to be artistic director. Then we can have some really good ballets."

"I like the programs the Boguslav puts on," I said.

"Haven't you noticed they never put on *The Bluebird,* or *Le Corsaire?* Or anything else that really shows my *élévation?*"

"Will you have time for dancing if you're artistic director?"

"I'll appear in a solo or a *pas de deux* at every performance. That won't take much rehearsal and it will guarantee a full house every time."

Alexander couldn't stand it any more. "What makes you think," he asked, "that you will be artistic director?"

"Viktor arranged it, of course. He wrote a letter to the board of directors. It has to be kept quiet, of course, but right after the Russian tour . . ."

"Have you seen this letter?" Alexander asked sceptically.

"I have one copy in my safe-deposit box and I keep another in my wallet. It's in his own handwriting."

"Why would Boguslav give you such a letter?"

"He had to. I told him I had some very good offers and there was no point in my staying around carrying the whole company if I didn't have my artistic freedom. So he promised that he would name me, upon his resignation."

"Or his death?"

"Well, of course. I didn't want there to be any loopholes."

"But suppose he didn't resign for years, Tindall? After all, he was only sixty-one."

"I didn't sign anything," Tindall said primly. "I wasn't going to wait around until I was twenty-five, you know. If he took too long to retire I would just have starred in another company and let the Boguslav rot."

"Then his death was a godsend to you?"

"Not just to me, Mr. Gold. To the company, to my fans, to dance. Take the finale of *Spectre of the Rose,* for instance," Tindall said heatedly. "Have you ever seen the Spirit of the Rose perform the final *grand jeté* through the back window with his body turned toward the Girl?"

"The dancers I've seen," I said, "have always faced in the direction of the leap. You could get killed doing such a big jump without seeing where you're landing."

"That's exactly what I mean. Nijinsky started his *grand jeté* facing forward, in the normal manner, and in mid-air he turned his torso completely around so he went through the window facing backward, toward the audience."

"I've heard of that. Wasn't he supposed to have cleared almost five feet?"

"No one ever measured, that's the trouble. I'm going to prove that I'm the only one who can jump higher than Nijinsky."

"I've heard that people who have seen them both dance say that Pierre equalled Nijinsky's *élévation,* and Pierre is even shorter than Nijinsky."

"Pure guesswork," said Kurt vehemently, "that's all it is. And if it ever did happen, it was twenty years ago. Today Pierre looks like he's glued to the floor. And even so, they all jumped over low window sills; I'm going to *prove* how high I can jump."

"Going to have a tape measure on stage?"

"I've been practicing in secret," he said smugly. "How would you like to see me do a *grand jeté,* reversing in mid-air, over a five-foot high wooden window sill, in perfect position?"

"I'd really love to see that," I said. I meant it too, even if he made it.

"Why do you think they didn't put me in *Graven Image?* Because in the jumping line scene, I would have made them all look sick. Do you know why Pierre, who was supposed to be the Leader, jumped last? Because if he had to do the forty-two jumps of the first in the line, he would have fainted right on stage."

"He looks pretty good to me on stage," I said, and I meant it. Only two years younger than Alexander, Pierre was still slim and muscular, and moved like a boy.

"You're an amateur," Tindall sneered. "You don't see what a dancer sees. He is clumsy and moves like lead. He can barely get off the ground. And he's ugly too, practically a dwarf; an ugly dwarf, that's what he is. It makes me sick just to look at him." Tindall, at maybe five-eight, was seven inches taller than Pierre; big deal. "The only reason Viktor kept him on," Tindall persisted, "was pity. No one else would hire him. Viktor told me so himself."

"You didn't, by any chance, let this little tidbit drop where Pierre could hear it, did you?" Alexander asked.

"Oh, he knew about it already," Tindall said smugly. "It was no secret in the company." I'll bet it wasn't, I thought; you saw to that.

"Where were you when Boguslav was killed?" Alexander asked.

"In here," he said. "Putting on makeup before the performance. From seven o'clock on."

"But you were doing the Moor," I said. "That doesn't take two hours. All you have to do is put on a black clown face."

"That's what everyone else does," he said with a superior smile. "You don't think I'm just going to smear on black, do you? And hide my features? I was trying out how I would look in light tan. Not all Moors are pure black, you know. That way my features would be visible."

"But the part is that of a doll," I protested. "You're supposed to look crudely made up." Wasted. Well, carry on. I asked, "Did you leave your dressing room? To watch *Graven Image,* for instance?"

"After it started I went backstage to let Zoris check my makeup. He's a real stick-in-the-mud, gets very nasty if you make the slightest improvement without asking him, but he wasn't backstage."

"Did you go up to the Grand Tier?"

"I may have; I really wasn't paying attention. Did anyone say they saw me there?"

"If you were made up heavily and wearing street clothes, you could wander anywhere in the theater and no one would recognize you."

"That's ridiculous, Mr. Gold, I am recognized by my fans

everywhere, even on the street. They know how I move."

"Did your tan Moor have a beard, Mr. Tindall?"

"I really don't remember, Mr. Gold. I tried many different combinations."

"Why would you want to kill Viktor Boguslav?"

"I don't have to kill anybody, Mr. Gold. If a person is not nice to me, he just doesn't exist for me. I avoid him."

"You couldn't avoid Viktor Boguslav."

"Of course I could. I could have gone to any other company. And been paid more. Much more."

"But then you wouldn't have been artistic director, would you? And you wouldn't have danced the *Blue Bird Variation,* would you? You thought you had tied down Viktor Boguslav, but he had you tied down instead. And once you were in his power, he could torture you by giving all the best roles to his lover, Pierre, a man old enough to be your father. Is that why you killed him, Kurt?"

"I didn't kill anyone," he burst out. "Pierre killed him. Pierre hated him because Viktor was making me artistic director. And Pierre knew that once I was in charge, I would throw him out and no one else would have him."

"The police think Jeffrey did it," Alexander said calmly.

"That's right," Kurt nodded vigorously. "Jeffrey helped Pierre. He let him in and held Viktor while Pierre killed him. Then he lied to the police about no one coming in."

"Why would Jeffrey help Pierre kill Boguslav?"

"They were lovers, Pierre and Jeffrey. Boguslav found out and was going to get rid of both of them."

"That's a real good solution," Alexander said. "There's only one minor problem. Pierre was on stage during *Graven Image* all the time."

"There were blackouts," Kurt said desperately. "All he had to do was run upstairs, kill Viktor, and run down again."

"Pretty fast work for a decrepit old man," Alexander pointed out. "And in that hairy costume with full stage makeup, he was taking a hell of a chance of being seen, wasn't he?"

"Maybe Jeffrey did it all by himself, but Pierre made him do it. Just put him in jail and make him confess."

Alexander was ready to do something unbeautiful to Kurt Tindall, so I changed the subject. "Do you wear boots in *Petrouchka?*"

"Well, of course. He's a Moor, isn't he?"

Alexander stood up to leave. "May I have a copy of the letter Boguslav gave you about being artistic director?"

Tindall looked shocked. "Certainly not."

"I didn't mean your copy," Alexander said. "I just want to make a copy of it. It doesn't even have to leave your hands; we'll just go into the office."

"What do you want it for?" Kurt asked.

"I'm going to show it to Max Baron," Alexander said, "so he can prepare the board of directors for your new position."

We got the copy and read it in the taxi on the way home. It was addressed to the Chairman of the Board of Directors.

Upon my resignation, whenever that may be, I hereby order the Board of Directors to elect, unanimously, Mr. Kurt Tindall, to be Artistic Director of the Boguslav Ballet Russe.

Mr. Tindall's great élévation and tremendous *ballon* have given me great pleasure. He has worked well under me, with great skill and talent, and I am sure the younger members of the *corps de ballet* will perform their required functions equally well under him. His firm grasp of all the elements that make a dancer give joy to all is second only to his capacity to encompass all that I have been able to pro-

vide him. Although much emphasis has been
placed upon his physical beauty, it must not be
forgotten that Kurt Tindall is not only a great
performer, but has shown that he can use his
head too. And while he may not be prone to sat-
isfy every member of the company, nor bend at
all times to anyone's idle whims, he is sufficiently flexible to take care of the individual or collective needs of most members. Further, I am sure that if any other openings
become available, Mr. Tindall will do his ut-
most to fill them and to handle any other posts
which come his way.
    With the greatest sincerity,
      Viktor Boguslav, General Manager

"He forgot to say 'over my dead body,' " I pointed out.

"He practically did, in his first sentence," Alexander replied.

"You really have to admire the bastard," I said. "Even
from the grave, he is screwing somebody."

"Well, he couldn't have done it to anyone else; Kurt was
practically begging for it. Boguslav wouldn't have dared to
try something like this on Tatiana."

"No, he screwed her a worse way, twenty years ago. I hope
you don't think that our jumping Narcissus is not capable
of murder."

"Come on, Norma, he could never in his life figure out
how to do it."

"No, but maybe someone figured it out for him. Maybe
we're wrong in looking for a single killer. If we think of two,
or even three of them working together, a lot of possibilities
open up."

"I already thought of a cooperative effort. Every one in-
volves Jeffrey."

I had to get him out of this mood, so I said, "Can you imagine Kurt Tindall reading this to the board of directors?"

The taxi driver couldn't figure out why we were laughing so crazily. Or was it hysterically?

21

"You mean," Burton asked, "you don't have even a suspicion of who did it?"

Burton and Pearl had come over after supper to check progress.

"Have a heart, Burt," Pearl said. "We've only been on it for two days. I think we've learned a lot."

"What, for instance?"

"Motive, means, and opportunity," I said. "Everybody, but everybody, had a motive to kill Boguslav. And everybody had the means, or at least it was possible for any one of them to buy that knife, grind it to a double edge, remove the handle, and hide it on him. Or her. And everybody had the opportunity, except Pierre."

"Wrong," Alexander said. "Just because he was in *Graven Image* doesn't mean he couldn't have killed Boguslav. And just because Tindall is in love with Tindall and hates Pierre, it doesn't necessarily mean he's wrong. There were several times when the stage was blacked out completely for at least a minute, and even close to two."

"He may have had the time," I said, "but how could he get to the box in full costume?"

"Easy," Alexander answered. "There were the stairs down to the orchestra at the end of the stage. He goes down the stairs, through a fire exit, up the fire stair and he's right next to the box."

"Can't work," I said. "If he opened the fire exit door, the light from the corridor would be seen by everyone in the theater."

"Then maybe he went out directly into the fire stair from the stage level. Remember, all the lights were out backstage. And," he raised his hand to stop my protest, "it would have been easy for him to loosen the light bulbs in the fire stair so that opening the door would not be noticed."

"Zoris and Spenser, even Jeffrey, didn't mention that the lights were out on the Grand Tier level when they took Boguslav up in the elevator," I said.

"No, but it would have been easy for Pierre to loosen the bulbs after they went up in the elevator."

"Someone would have noticed later."

"In the confusion after the killing, he could have run up the stairs and turned the bulbs on again. These dancers are very fast; no one would have noticed his absence for that minute."

"But he would have to enter the corridor in full costume. Someone might have seen him."

"He could have covered the distance from the stair to the box in one or two seconds. In fact, he could have peeked out to see if anyone was there first."

"Alexander," I asked, "do you really think Pierre did it?"

"I didn't say he did it; I just don't want to rule him out yet."

"Great," Burton said. "So all six of your suspects had motives, means, and opportunity. I can use that when the case comes to trial."

"Not so good for us," I said, to prevent Alexander from saying something stronger. "First, if any one of them did it, it could only have been done with the cooperation of Jeffrey Baron, which leaves us down one hundred grand. Second, if Warshafsky thinks one of them did it, and doesn't know which one, he'll hold the troupe here while he investigates, which still leaves us down a hundred. Even if he limits himself to holding only those six, the Russian trip will be called off. Again, minus one hundred."

"Can't they get a substitute for whoever did it?" Pearl asked.

"Probably, if we could prove to Warshafsky's satisfaction who it was. But all six? Never."

"I have some more news for you, which I wasn't going to tell you," said Burton, "but now, I might as well."

I steeled myself for more bad news. Alexander looked beaten. Whatever it was, I didn't want to hear it.

"The State Department is anxious for the Russian tour to go ahead," Burton said.

"Why?" Alexander asked. "They have spies in the entourage?"

"Probably," Burton replied. "But they are also trying to strengthen those Russians who are pushing for cultural exchanges and easing relations between us and them."

"Good," I said. "Tell them to pressure Warshafsky to let the company go."

"What they are doing," Burton said, "is pressuring the commissioner to make Warshafsky arrest Jeffrey. So far, Warshafsky is resisting, but I don't know how much longer he can hold out."

"It all boils down to what I said from the start," Alexander said. "I have to find the real killer. Let's stop fooling around and get down to analysis." He turned to Pearl. "Do you have any diagrams or photos of the body?"

"No, but I have a good description. The wheelchair was

exactly where Spenser and Zoris had put it, with its footrest against the end wall of the box, in the corner, with the right wheel ten inches from the front wall."

Alexander blew his top. "Why doesn't anybody tell me these things?" he yelled. "How the hell am I supposed to solve this case if everybody sits on important information? My time is two thirds gone and now, NOW, I find this out? All you told me before was that they spent a long time putting him into the exact position he wanted. You didn't tell me he wasn't facing center stage. What else is everybody keeping from me?"

"Alexander," I tried to soothe him, "nobody is keeping anything from you. Pearl has been working practically all alone. She's put together a tremendous amount of information; so much that she might have lost sight of what she gave you or didn't give you."

"The why didn't Burton give it to me? Didn't I ask for the complete police files?"

"It's not so easy to get police files, Alec," Burton said. "The best I could do was to get parts read to me over the phone. If you'll just calm down I'll tell you everything I know about the body, and the chair."

Alexander didn't answer, just waved Burton to talk. Pearl switched on the recorder she's learned to carry at all times.

"Boguslav's wheelchair," Burton said, "was specially designed for him, bigger and stronger, to carry his size and weight. It had two batteries instead of one, and the legs and back could be tilted electrically to any position from full recline to upright. It could travel forward and backward at about two miles per hour, and could turn in a five-foot radius. The wheels and the rests could be moved by hand if the batteries ran down.

"Boguslav was sitting, as he always did, with his legs

straight out, the chair's footrest tight against the end wall of the box, right in the corner nearest the stage center. Due to the slight angle of the end wall, and the curvature of the front wall, the hub of the right wheel was almost ten inches from the front wall on his right, and he was facing at almost right angles to the stage. The backrest was tilted back at almost exactly forty-five degrees. Boguslav's arms were hanging loosely at his sides."

Alexander eyed us in disgust. "Do you know how important this is?" he asked. "If I had known this from the beginning . . . For all I know, I may have completely wasted the last two days."

"Well, why didn't you stick your head through the curtain?" I asked. "Then you would have seen everything and could have solved the case right then and there."

"Same reason you didn't," he said. "Because Max Baron snapped the curtain shut and wouldn't let anyone near it until the police came. He thought he was helping Jeffrey."

"I don't see how the position of the wheelchair matters that much," Pearl said.

Anytime Alexander gets a captive audience to explain things to, he becomes nice, especially if it's an attractive female. "Was the chair tilted back when Boguslav was pushed into position?" he asked.

"No," Pearl said. "I would have mentioned it if it had."

"Okay," Alexander settled into his chair. "With the chair tilted back, Boguslav's head had to be at about the height of the railing on top of the front wall of the box. This would make it almost impossible for him to watch the ballet, so it's highly improbable that Boguslav tilted it back himself. Jeffrey? Before the killer came in? If so, did Jeffrey decide to do it on his own or did Boguslav ask him to? And if Jeffrey did it and didn't tell me, I will kill him slowly. But why should Boguslav ask Jeffrey to do this? If the chair was motorized, there had to be a switch for going forward and back, another for raising and lowering the legrest, and one for raising and lowering the back. Right, Pearl?"

"The knob for turning the chair was on the left armrest," Pearl said, "and the three switches were on the right armrest."

"Exactly," Alexander nodded, "and I'll bet they were on a little panel next to each other about an inch apart. And that the driving control was on the inside, while the back control was on the outside, or at worst, in the middle."

"I don't know," Pearl said, "but I'll check it."

"Anyway, we can be sure that Boguslav wouldn't push the switch to move his backrest so he couldn't see the new ballet. And why should Boguslav call Jeffrey to push a little switch? Especially after telling Jeffrey to stay in the cloakroom? Answer, he didn't. So if neither Jeffrey nor Boguslav did it, who did?"

"The killer," I said. "But I can't imagine why."

"Or when," Alexander said. "Visualize this. The killer walks through the curtain. He is directly behind Boguslav's head. He leans over Viktor's right shoulder and whispers, 'Hello, Viktor, you dirty rat, I've come to kill you.' He puts his left hand across Boguslav's mouth, reaches down with his right hand and stabs Boguslav in the heart. Right? Wrong!"

"Maybe Boguslav pulled the switch back after he was stabbed," I suggested.

"So when did the killer pull out Boguslav's blouse to wrap around the knife handle?"

"All right," I said. "It's obvious that the killer stood to the right of the wheelchair, between the chair and the front wall of the box. He pulls out the blouse and then stabs Boguslav. In the act of pulling out the blouse, he pushes the tilt switch back."

"With which hand?"

"With his right hand, naturally," I said. "He's standing facing Boguslav, his right hand is toward Boguslav's feet. I see. That's why you said that the back-tilt switch was probably the outer switch, though it wouldn't matter if it was the middle, since the legrest was up anyway."

"Correct. Now in which hand was the knife?"

"In his left hand. Actually he was holding the knife by the nylon loop to avoid fingerprints."

"Great, Norma," he said sarcastically. "The killer walks through the curtain and squeezes in between the front wall of the box and the wheelchair, why we don't know yet. He has the knife in his left hand, by the loop. He pulls out Boguslav's blouse with his right hand and puts that hand under the blouse bottom ready to receive the knife. Meanwhile he accidentally tilts the chair back forty-five degrees. He then lays the knife on the blouse over his right hand in exactly the proper position for the knife to be held, lays his left hand over Boguslav's mouth to stifle any screams, and stabs Boguslav. And during all this, Boguslav says nothing? Does nothing? Hah!"

"All right," said Burton. "So how was it done?"

"I don't know yet," Alexander replied. "But you can see how little bits of information can be important. If I had known this earlier, I might have looked along other lines. And there are other questions too. Why did Boguslav insist on being placed in this exact position? Shouldn't he have faced center stage?"

"I know that," said Pearl. "Because if he were facing center, he would be several feet away from the wall of the box, his feet would be sticking out, and he wouldn't have been able to see the front of the stage. This way, he could look to the right over the wall and see practically everything."

"Then why wasn't the chair put right next to the wall of the box, with the wheel touching the wall? That way he could look over the wall more easily and see the whole stage. No, there was some good reason, some pattern, which connects all these clues. Here we have several things that are seemingly unrelated: the little knife with two sharp edges, no handle, and a nylon loop; the peculiar position of the wheelchair; the blouse tucked into the pants, and later pulled out; the tilt of the wheelchair's back; the unusual angle of stabbing. And through all these operations, the silence of Boguslav is unexplained; not one sound, which we would have heard through the curtain, even through the music. Yet they all have to fit; they are all part of the pattern of what actually happened. When I figure out how they fit, I'll have the killer."

"Alexander," I said, having to say it even knowing what would happen, "all of this sounds impossible if you assume the killer had to get past Jeffrey and had to have four hands to do all these things at once. But the killer plus Jeffrey have four hands . . ."

Alexander looked at me with real fury. "Don't ever say that to me again," he said, very quietly, too quietly. "Jeffrey did *not* kill Boguslav. Jeffrey did not *help* kill Boguslav. Jeffrey is innocent. And the only way to prove it is to keep that in mind. Anything else and my mind will go along the wrong channels and that will be the end. I don't want to be influenced by negative ideas. Is that clear? When I go to sleep tonight, my subconscious will start with the knowledge, the absolute certainty, that Jeffrey is innocent. It will then reveal the answer to the puzzle and I will have the killer."

"Then you better go to sleep early," Burton said. "You only have twenty-four hours left."

"Wrong," said Alexander. "I have twenty-seven hours. It's only nine o'clock and I have till midnight Sunday."

Burton looked concerned. "But Alexander, you misunderstood. The plane is scheduled to leave at midnight. But the troupe and the baggage, costumes, everything, they have to be at the airport at 9:30, to be checked and searched. You know, subversive literature and things like that; these are Russians we're dealing with. And you have to figure an hour to get to Kennedy, in case of a traffic tieup, a flat, or whatever."

Alexander glowered. "I was promised till midnight Sunday. You can't change the rules on me now."

"I'm not changing the rules, Alec," Burton said gently. "I want exactly what you want. But this is how things are. I'll help all I can; just tell me what you want and I'll get it."

"Just give me all the facts," he snapped. "That's all I want. I'm going to the office to think. Don't disturb me."

After an hour, I disturbed him. I couldn't help it, visualizing him agonizing over this impossible problem, this insoluble puzzle, that had to be solved by nine o'clock tomorrow night. I had to do what any good wife would do; let Alexander drop the case in such a way that it would look as though it were entirely my fault.

I went into the office without knocking. Alexander was stretched out on his recliner, staring at the ceiling, but his face was tense and his hands were clenched.

"Alexander," I said, "I want to talk to you. Seriously." He kept staring at the ceiling, a bad sign.

"Alexander, this is a ridiculous case. Jeffrey holds back information; for all we know, he is still holding back, or even lying. The others? What have they told you that is of any use? All they've said is that they didn't do it and that everybody else hated Boguslav. And there's the physical problem. No one could have done it except Jeffrey. Or, if someone else did the actual killing, it had to be with Jeffrey's knowledge and assistance."

He was silent for a moment, then, eyes still fixed on the ceiling, spoke. "Thank you for explaining my problem to me."

"I wasn't rubbing it in, darling," I said soothingly. "I was just trying, preparing myself, for what I have to say. Let me go on." I hesitated for a moment, trying to find the best approach. Whatever I did, or did not do, I had to avoid exciting him, turning this discussion into a quarrel between us. "Do you remember, when we were first married, how poor we were? We were so happy. I used to worry at night that it could change. And when we were building up your consulting practice? How hard we worked, how we counted every penny, and yet, how happy we were?"

He turned to look at me. "I've always been happy with you, Norma. Because of you."

"Exactly, Alexander. As long as we have each other, nothing else is important. Now that we have some money invested, are we any happier than before?"

"We're a hell of a lot more secure. If anything happens to me, you're taken care of. That's important to me."

"This case could kill you," I said bluntly. "I don't want to be a rich widow. Between us, we can always make a living."

"No," he said firmly.

"Yes, Alexander," I said gently. "I don't care about the hundred thousand dollars. I want you to sleep next to me tonight with a clear head."

"It's not just the money, Norma. Please don't ask me."

"Remember, Alexander, you once promised me, that if I ever wanted you to do something, really wanted it, and I asked you, you would do it. No arguments; you would just do it. Well, I want you to drop this case."

"I can't."

"You feel a responsibility to Jeffrey? That little jerk isn't worth the effort. And that's assuming that he's completely innocent, which I doubt."

"He's innocent, Norma, although I'm not sure how completely, and any innocent person is worth the effort. But what about his father? And his mother? They came from a concentration camp. Do I let them down?"

"Between them and you? I pick you."

"All right. How about the thousand Jews. Do I get them out of Russia?"

"Is it worth risking your life for, Alexander?"

"If not me, who?"

I had lost. Or gained. I'm not sure which. "All right, Alexander. What are you going to do?"

"I'm going over the case from all angles. Then while I sleep, my subconscious will put everything in the proper pattern."

I brought him some strong hot cocoa and a Dalmane. His subconscious had a lot of work to do this night; something stronger than Valium was called for.

22

When I woke up on Sunday morning, Alexander was lying flat on his back, eyes open, not moving. My heart clenched and for a moment I thought—, but then he blinked. He was deep in concentration, so I feigned sleep, not to disturb him.

When I got up he was already dressed. Smiling. Good old subconscious; always there when you need it. As I dressed he told me we were going to Brodsky's Gym to talk to Danilo Hurkos.

"Why Danilo?" I asked. "He couldn't have done it."

"He could have helped," Alexander said. "Since I am sure Jeffrey isn't involved, the killer had to have come from outside the box. That means the stage. It's obvious."

Danilo Hurkos, in a faded blue sweatsuit and looking positively beautiful, had just started a heavy workout when we got there. I could tell that Alexander was dying to join him, but the doctor had said that it would be another month before Alexander could go back to the gym.

"I want to compliment you on your performance in *Graven Image*," I said. "If I hadn't known otherwise, I would have thought you had been on the stage all of your life."

"In a sense I have," he answered, not breathing hard, although he was doing alternate presses with a hundred-pound dumbbell in each hand. "In body-building contests, presentation is half the battle. There are men with bigger measurements than I have, or more classic proportions, or better definition, but I've learned how to pose to maximum advantage, how to move gracefully into and out of poses, how to walk, how to have a relaxed smile with tense muscles, and, most important, how to stand still and look good. It's very much the same as ballet."

"How did you like working with that company?" I asked.

"Wonderful. It was a revelation. Those kids are great athletes. I'll bet half the guys in this gym couldn't keep up with them. And they're strong, too. Did you see the thighs on Tindall? Almost as big as mine. And the build on that little Pierre? At his age? If he had taken up weightlifting instead of ballet, he could have given Isaac Berger a run for the money, and old Ike was the best lifter of his time, pound for pound."

"Did the homosexuality bother you?"

"Mrs. Gold," he said, "anytime you get a bunch of good-looking young men in one place, ballet or body-building contests or theater, you're going to have people around who like handsome young men. You either do or you don't; no one twists your arm."

"I take it you don't," I said.

"If that's what you were trying to find out, you could have asked me directly, Mrs. Gold. No, I'm strictly hetero."

"I'll bet you have lots of attractive young women hanging around too."

"Young and old, attractive and not-so. Like any sport, only more so here. I used to love it; imagine, when I was twenty, all those girls—, every day—.But it gets—, you find that it's not what you really want. What I want, I'm thirty now, is to have a normal life, in one place, a home, a wife, a family."

"What will you do, now that you're retiring?"

"I've saved most of my money and I'm going to start a business. But for the next year I'll go to school, take some postgrad courses in modern economic theory."

"Why economics?"

"I've seen that every new economic theory has failed, that economists, and the governments that use them, are not only wrong but they don't seem to learn from reality, they stick to their theories. So when I go into business, I'll do the opposite of what current theory advises, and I should do very well. But first I have to understand the theory."

This young man was a definite possible; what did I have to lose? "The wife you mentioned, does she have to be any specific type? Blond or brunette? Tall or short? Rich or poor? Fat or thin?"

"Mrs. Gold, when I meet her, if I like her and she likes me, then I'll know what she looks like. But," he added gallantly, "if she's anything like you . . . If I were ten years older, your husband would have a rival."

I think I may have blushed a little. "I know a girl who is just like me," I said, remembering what Pearl had said. "Would you like to meet her?"

"Sure," he said. "Make it a formal introduction please, not just a phone number."

"I'll have a party right after the Russian tour. Which is definitely on." I turned to Alexander, "I think."

Alexander, who had been waiting impatiently, took his cue. "Mr. Hurkos," he asked, "how high could you throw a hundred-pound dumbbell?"

Danilo stared at him for a moment, then his face cleared. "Mr. Gold, it's impossible. You look like a lifter, here is a hundred pounder; you try it."

Alexander looked embarrassed. "I've just had a bad heart attack," he said. "I'm not allowed any stress. Besides I'm a powerlifter; we do slow movements."

"Well," Danilo said, "I can tell you that I couldn't throw that barbell more than a foot or so straight up, at the most. And it's rigid. Imagine if I tried to throw a person, who is flexible and would absorb the push, and be hard to balance as well. And the smallest man there must weigh at least one-twenty."

"Betsy Gilman can't weigh more than ninety pounds, and Tatiana is surely not over one hundred."

"Even so, Mr. Gold. Figure it out. I have Betsy Gilman standing on my hands. My palms are less than seven feet, six inches above the floor. She's not even five feet tall, so she reaches less than six feet, six inches. So we start at less than fourteen feet. Even if I could throw her two feet up and some distance forward, that's still only sixteen feet. That balcony must be twenty feet up."

"A little over seventeen feet," Alexander said. "Okay. One man can't. How about two men? Swinging her. Like adagio dancers."

Danilo thought for a while. "I don't think so, Mr. Gold. I have never seen adagio dancers but I know what you mean. It looks as though the girl is flying high in the air, but actually, she's no higher than a foot or so from the outstretched hands. The swing starts from ground level, that's why it looks so big." He thought for a while longer, then added, "And when was it done? Not when everyone could see. In the dark? I wouldn't let myself be thrown into space in the dark. And who helped me? The tallest man in the troupe is shorter than I am. And why would I do it? I had no reason to kill Mr. Boguslav."

"Everyone else did," Alexander said, clearly miffed at the failure of his solution. "Why not you?"

"I had a very good relationship with Mr. Boguslav," Danilo said. "I helped him in many ways, and he appreciated it."

"How did you help him?"

"The belts, for instance. He wanted to have them fastened with a clip in the back that would come apart easily for quick costume changes. I asked him how he would like to see one of his dancers flying out into the audience when a clip opened up. We ended up with a belt continuous around the body with a friction clamp buckle that the belt could slide through easily if the tension were off."

"That makes sense," said Alexander. "What else?"

"The big decorative buckles in front. He was going to have them big round circles six inches in diameter made of one-inch stock. I told them there was no way anyone could hold a bunch of these in his hands. That's when we changed to smaller D-shaped ones, so I could have a straight portion to hold. Then I had him increase the number of dancers from twelve to fourteen."

"Wouldn't that make it harder to hold?"

"Easier. Try holding six pencils together in your hand; they don't make an even grip. But seven, that's six around one, forms a perfectly stable cylinder. Then I reduced the diameter of the stock to three eighths of an inch."

"That's the size you're used to holding," Alexander said.

"Right. Barbells are one and an-eighth inches in diameter, and a cluster of seven three-eighths-inch bars is exactly the same. Then Mr. Boguslav, he was going to do that role before the accident, was going to have a pair of grips connected by a strap across his back to hold the dancers. I showed him there was no way a mechanical grip could be sure of releasing all the dancers at the same time for the big finale when they all jumped up and turned around to wrap the belts around them. It has to be done by hand. And the problem is not the pull across my body, it's the unbalanced pull at right angles to my arms. I asked Mr. Ziladiev to put his best dancers in that position, front and back, and to train them not to pull more than a certain amount. If they felt themselves swinging away from me, they had to slack off quickly."

"And Ziladiev listened to you?"

"When he saw I was right, he did. Those guys are real pros; even handed me the buckles in the right order."

"So you had no quarrel with Boguslav at all?"

"We argued about money, sure. He wanted me to do it for minimum, for the publicity. I told him that, as Mr. Galaxy seven times running, undefeated, I was getting *him* publicity, as well as new customers. Then he promised he would star me in two new ballets, he even had the names: *Samson and Delilah,* and *The Seven Labors of Hercules.* I told him we would discuss them after he signed the contract for *Graven Image.* I was practically the only one he could use and we both knew it."

"Other than that, no problems? He didn't press you for sexual relations?"

"Of course he did. Everybody does. Not for me, but because I'm Mr. Galaxy. That's one of the things that turned me off groupies. I don't make a big deal; I just say no."

In the taxi on the way home, Alexander sat silent. He had his unfocussed look, staring at nothing, deep thought. When we got home he headed straight for his office. He leaned all the way back in his recliner and stared at the ceiling. I closed the door gently and went into Pearl's room to check progress. Nothing worthwhile, at least as far as I could see, but Pearl was typing reports, just in case, to avoid another outburst from Alexander when he would accuse us of withholding obviously vital facts from him.

The intercom suddenly squawked. "Pearl," Alexander said, "I need the military experience of each suspect."

Pearl had that at her fingertips. "Ziladiev was in the Free French forces under de Gaulle. In England; never saw action. Romanoff seems to have been in the Resistance in Paris with his older sister, although he was not quite eleven when the war ended. Spenser was a schoolboy who volunteered for the Home Guard, and did some coast watching. Tatiana was first born when World War II ended and never served in any military organization. Betsy was never in any military organization either. Tindall was in high school ROTC for one year."

A moment later, Alexander came into Pearl's office. He looked excited and upset. "Norma, there's something in my memory. I don't know what, can't put my finger on it. When

I was in cardiac arrest it must have destroyed some brain cells. I need a library, a big one. You're a librarian, what would be open on Sunday?"

"Nothing. Not even Forty-second Street."

"Pearl, tell Max Baron to get a library opened for me. Fast."

"Alexander," I said, "don't be foolish. *God* couldn't get the New York City bureaucracy to move fast. But college libraries could be open."

"Great, Norma. Find me one and get me in, with permission to search all stacks."

"I don't have to find," I said. "I know. Yeshivah University Library is guaranteed open on Sunday. Pearl, is Max Baron a big contributor to Yeshivah?"

"Of course. I'll call him now; you two get started."

"I don't need you, Norma," he said. "Stay here and wait till you hear from Warshafsky. Then find me quick."

"But I'm a librarian," I protested.

"That only helps when you know what you're looking for. I'll be looking at random, and only I will be able to recognize it when I find it." He took off in a hurry.

The race was on; ten hours to go.

23

Our talk with Danilo Hurkos had given me an idea, so I called Lou Attell. "I need information," I told him.

"Two days," he said, "and the case isn't solved yet? Al must be losing his grip."

I love to kid with Lou; he's one of the few engineers I know who is literate, but the meter was ticking, so I got right down to business. "In *A Night at the Opera*, Harpo Marx was swinging around the stage on ropes. Do they still do that these days?"

"Certainly. About half the theaters in New York are 'hemp houses.' Ropes are more flexible, in many ways, than the counterweight system."

"How does it work?"

"When you want to fly a drop, that is, lift or lower a curtain which acts as part of the scenery, you attach ropes to the top bar which holds the drop. These ropes go up to pulleys fixed to the gridiron, a steel or wooden framework high above the stage. The ropes then go to another set of pulleys over the fly floor where they are fastened to the belaying pins on the pin rail. By pulling or releasing these ropes, you can lift the drops or lower them. For heavy drops, sandbags are sometimes used as counterweights."

"Are these ropes strong enough to support a person, Lou? Could someone swing from where the ropes are tied to Boguslav's box?"

"The ropes are tied to drops, Norma. You untie a line and swing from it, either you or the drop ends up on the stage. They're made to go up and down, not in and out."

"If a rope were not attached to a drop, Lou . . . What if someone, a week earlier, say, attached a rope to the gridiron when no one was around, and tied it to the pins. Couldn't he swing out to Boguslav's box, kill Boguslav, and then swing back? During one of the blackouts?"

"I haven't explained enough, Norma," he said. "First of all, every rope is carefully marked. A stagehand would notice an extra rope right away. Second, you seem to be under the impression that the fly floor and the ropes are at the back of the stage. They're not. They're at the side of the stage, deep in the wings."

"Which side, Lou? In the Temple Theater, I mean."

"Stage right. Which is where the left side of the audience is."

"That's where Boguslav's box is, Lou. Couldn't someone have swung out and around to Boguslav's box?"

"Positively not." He sounded regretful. "The fly floor is thirty feet above the stage and over twenty feet behind the proscenium arch. Then, the house curtain was kept open about six feet, more or less in line with the end of the box, to narrow the stage. The pin rail, where the ropes are tied, is about four feet above the fly floor. You'd have to swing out about thirty feet, to clear the curtain, with your feet about thirty feet above the stage, and swing back to the middle of the Boguslav box—figure about thirteen feet from the end of the curtain and seventeen feet above the stage. Impossible."

"Couldn't a trained athlete do it? Or a ballet dancer?"

"Norma, you're so worried, you're not thinking straight. Let's say the killer got up to the gridiron, which is about ninety feet up, and tied a rope there, after making a calculation of the exact location. Let's say he even tested it with a sandbag. Assume further that no stagehand noticed the strange rope, and these are guys who scream to the union if an actor accidently moves a flat. The killer has to get up to the fly floor unnoticed. He waits for a blackout, unties the rope, stands on the pin rail, and swings out. He figured correctly and one second later he finds himself over the middle of Boguslav's box. One hundredth of a second later, CRUNCH, he's smeared against the back wall of the box."

"Suppose he kept his feet out," I said desperately, "to cushion the impact?"

"Okay," Lou said amiably. "He keeps his feet out and is so skillful that he lands with his feet against the wall, instead of his empty head. He finds he is now twenty feet above the floor of the box. Cleverly, he slides down the rope, being careful not to land on Boguslav, who is approximately the size of the box. He finds Boguslav in the dark by feel, and stabs him. Meanwhile, Boguslav doesn't say one word? Now the killer has to swing back to the fly floor, otherwise there will be an unexplained rope lousing up the next scene. The fly floor tie rail is twenty feet higher than where he is standing and twenty feet farther back. And all this is done in total darkness. Even Tarzan couldn't do it."

I don't give up that easily. "Suppose after he kills Boguslav he slides down the rope and swings a little to land on the stage, which is only a few feet from the end of the box. Then he runs up to the fly floor, taking the rope with him. Wouldn't that work?"

"Norma, do you know what backstage looks like during a scene change? How would you like to drag a three-quarter-inch Manila rope through a Fortunoff's sale, and *schlepp* it up a thirty-foot ladder in ten seconds in total darkness? Tarzan? Hell, even Cheetah couldn't do it."

Well, it was a good idea while it lasted. The only thing left to do was to review the transcripts of the taped interviews and see if I could find a discrepancy. I settled down in Alexander's recliner with the files and a box of Barton's chocolate cherries. The brain needs an awful lot of glucose for heavy thinking. Mine does, anyway.

I found it by the third cherry. Amazing. No one had noticed it but me; not even Alexander. I checked forward; it was true. Right in front of everyone's eyes, practically obvious, and only I had caught it. But I had to verify it, first.

Fortunately, Jeffrey was home. I had to phrase my questions carefully. "How did you arrange the chairs in the cloakroom area of the box?" I asked.

"I put the first one against the end wall for my head," Jeffrey answered, "and the rest touching each other."

"Your shoulders were on the second chair, your bottom on the third, and your feet on the fourth?"

"My feet overhung the end of the last chair so that I could lie flat. My calves were on the end chair."

"Were the backs of the chair legs against the step leading down into the box?" I tried not to sound tense.

"I don't think so. Why?"

I hung up, triumphant. Alexander would turn green with envy. Even if the chairs were as little as one inch away from the step, almost anyone could have slipped through the door of the box without Jeffrey's knowledge or cooperation. Wait till Alexander got home, would he *plotz*. But why wait? I'd call.

There was no answer at the Yeshivah Library. Either he wasn't answering the phone, or had left in frustration. How he even dreamed that he could find one obscure fact in those tens of thousands of books . . . It had to be desperation. Or panic. No matter. When he came home I would tell him what I had discovered and he'd fall on his knees and kiss the ground I walked on. I might even save one chocolate cherry for him, as a reward for acting nice. If he did.

He didn't. I had given Pearl the tapes of my two phone calls to transcribe and just gotten back to my office, when Alexander dashed in. Before I even kissed him I said, "Darling, I just found out that the killer couldn't swing into Boguslav's box by the backstage ropes."

"Of course not," he said, as I helped him off with his coat. "I never considered it. What I . . ."

"But I also found out," I interrupted, "that Jeffrey doesn't know if he put the chairs tightly against the stair in the box. In a few minutes Pearl will put together the excerpts of the transcripts that will show you this."

As I expected, it stopped him, but only for a few seconds. Then he dismissed the idea. "It's interesting, Norma, I'm glad you found it, but it's useless."

"Useless, Alexander? What about all the time we spent proving that only a skinny ballerina could have slipped into the box?"

"If a jury believes him, which is doubtful, it might get him off. But it's useless for our needs. What I was trying to tell you when you interrupted me was that I've solved the case."

"You *solved* the case?" I must have sounded like an idiotic echo. "How?"

"As soon as I knew who did it, I knew immediately how it was done."

"But you always said that when you figured out how it was done, you would know who did it."

"Precisely. When I knew how Boguslav was killed, I knew who did it, and as soon as I knew who did it, I knew how the murder was committed."

"Alexander, you're talking in circles again."

"No I'm not. Want to bet?"

"Don't play games with me, Alexander, I'm too nervous. Just explain."

"No time. Just do what I tell you; we have very little time. Call up Max Baron. I don't care how he does it, but I want a performance of *Graven Image* at the Temple Theater tonight. They have to leave for the airport by 8:30 so make it for 7 PM. Full costume, sets, orchestra, the works. Everything and everybody there just as it was on the night of the murder."

I gasped. "You can't do that, Alexander. Elly Ameling is giving a recital tonight. Her fans would tear you apart for even suggesting she cancel. If I had tickets, I would join them." So would Alexander; he is as crazy about the great Dutch soprano as I am.

"Elly?" he said. "We can't disturb *her.* All right, make it 6:45 and arrange that no one is allowed into the theater for her recital until 7:45. We'll just have to work a little faster, that's all."

"What are you talking about, Alexander?" I protested. "You can't put on a production on five minutes' notice. Everything is packed away. The lighting isn't set up, the costumes, the sets. It can't be done."

"For enough money, anything can be done."

"Whose money, Alexander? We have to eat all the costs. Do you know what this could run to? Thousands. Tens of thousands! We can't afford it, Alexander."

"We'll pay for it out of the million dollars I win."

"You're sure you'll win? Absolutely positive?"

"It's the only way it could have been done. It had to be that way."

"You're *phumpha-ing,* Alexander. Tell me it's a sure thing. Please. Tell me, Alexander."

He was silent for a moment, then spoke carefully. "It's not a sure thing, Norma, but I know I'm right."

I gave in; what choice does a wife have? "All right, Alexander, I'll do what you want. But let's cut some costs. Do you really need the whole orchestra?"

"I can do without it, if there's a tape of the performance. But there will have to be amplifiers and speakers."

"Okay. Do you need the sets?"

"Not really, I can do without them."

"Good. Now do you need the whole troupe?"

"Actually I need only the cast of *Graven Image,* plus the people we interviewed, and the backstage people, the dressers and the like. But they all have to be in the places they were, or claimed to be, on the night of the murder. And in full makeup and wearing the same clothes they were wearing then."

"Better yet. How about the lighting?"

He thought for a while. "The backstage lights, the footlights, and one spot; I can live with that. Set the spot in the center box of the Grand Tier."

I went into my office and got to work. Actually, I phoned Max Baron and told him to arrange it, with Pearl listening in. I told her to follow up every half hour and to nag everyone and to call me if there were any problems my whole bank account and overdraft couldn't handle.

When I went into Alexander's office I heard him on the telephone saying, ". . . got to have extra costumes lying around; have one altered. If not, make one from scratch. You told me you were resourceful, so be resourceful. Get it done and done properly. And on time; your life depends on it. By six o'clock. And don't forget the notepaper. My office. Goodby." He turned to me and said, "That was Jeffrey."

"So I gathered. Why didn't you give the budding impresario the whole schmeer to set up?"

"Because his job is critical and I don't want to overload him."

"I came to ask about an audience. You don't want one, do you?"

He looked shocked at the idea. "Positively not. I'm doing something delicate; it can't work with an audience."

"By you half a ballet company is not an audience?"

"I'll take care of them."

"Well, do you want the Barons and us in the box next to the Boguslav box?"

He looked away for a moment, then made the decision. "No, none of the Barons; not even Jeffrey."

"So, if you're recreating the conditions of the murder, who's going to sleep across the door to the box?"

"You will. You're about Jeffrey's height."

"Is that safe, Alexander?"

"Of course, Norma. You'll be perfectly safe."

I didn't like the way he worded that. "Does that mean *you'll* be in danger?"

"There may be a slight possibility; you can't say one hundred percent no in situations like this. But it's highly improbable. I can take care of myself."

Sure, like in the Talbott Case where he was trying to get himself shot instead of me. So guess who ended up in the hospital with two bullets in her belly? "And where will you be, hero?" I asked.

"In Boguslav's box, of course. In a wheelchair. Get me one, nothing fancy." Good. At least I could keep an eye on him there. And if anyone tried to sneak in past me, he'd get a big surprise, and it wouldn't be a seven-inch knife either, but whatever I could fit into my bag. My big bag. "And whatever happens," he said, "whatever happens, don't interfere." I nodded twice. By me, two positives make a negative.

Then it finally sank in. "Alexander, if all the house lights are out, there will be no light in the box, especially in the cloak area."

"Well, a little light will filter in from the stage."

"And the corridor outside the box will be totally dark too?"

"Totally."

"So what's to stop the killer from sneaking up the stairs to the box to get rid of you? Especially if he thinks you know who he is."

"Exactly," he smirked. "When he tries to open the door, we've got him."

"We've got *him*? Alexander, maybe he's got *me*. What if he's got another knife?"

"First he's got to lift the latch. Tie a thread from the latch to your hand. If you feel the latch lifting, scream. I'll be at him in one second; you know how fast I can react."

"Alexander, you're using your own loving wife for bait?"

That really got to him. He looked ashamed; the great planner had overlooked something. "Norma, I would never —It never occurred to me that you would be in the slightest danger. I thought I was taking all the risk. But you're right, there is a possibility that it could happen the way you said. You sit in the center box with the spotlight and the monitors. I'll tie a bell to the latch and put some weights on the chairs."

"Can Pearl be in the box with me? She deserves it. Also Burton." He looked doubtful, then nodded. "And Warshafsky? You going to invite the cops?"

"Naturally. Tell Warshafsky to bring two big plainclothesmen. Strong ones. I'll tell him where to place them later. Warshafsky will be in the center box too, with the stenographer."

"Which stenographer?"

"Isn't it obvious? We're going to need a court stenographer and a videotaper, the works, just like last time. Two videotapers, one camera in the center box of the Grand Tier to take in the whole stage and one in the Barons' box, shooting the Boguslav box through a hole in the curtain. And a bullhorn."

"Alexander," I said desperately, knowing he was in one of his Alexander the Great, Mighty-Emperor-Order-Giver moods, "there's a matinee on Sunday. The theater won't empty out until 5:15 at the earliest, maybe 5:30. We'll never get everything set up by 6:45. And Warshafsky, by the time he finishes with his kids and calls in, it will be six o'clock, at least. And two cops? There must be fifty ways to get out of that building. Do you *want* the killer to escape?"

"Don't worry," he waved away my objections. "I have everything planned." When Alexander tells me not to worry, that's the time to start worrying. "Send Pearl in," he said. I stuck my head outside the door and yelled; let her get her seven impossible labors now.

"I need a crooked ballet critic," he told her.

Pearl looked shocked. "But Alex," she said, "where? There aren't any. I never even heard of one, any of them, changing, even slanting, a review for money or favors or sex or anything."

He looked at her in disbelief, but she didn't budge, and since she had friends in all the arts and all the media, he couldn't argue with her. "All right," he gave in, "I'll handle it myself. I'll get Charles Augustine, he has a sense of humor; I could tell from *Graven Image*. Is Burton home?" Pearl nodded.

Alexander picked up the phone and dialled. "Burt? Alec. Everything's right on schedule. I just need one more thing: a forger. Come on, Burt, don't tell me . . . All right," he gave in, "a person who has wrongfully been accused of allegedly writing another person's name on a check without permission of said person. An expert. Yes. Right now. Here. Okay, any reasonable fee. No checks? Burton, do you think I would be so stupid as to give this alleged perpetrator one of my checks with my signature on it? Done. Thanks."

He got into his recliner and leaned all the way back, eyes closed, ready to sleep, resting up before the big game. Why should he worry? Norma and Pearl, ably assisted by: one billionaire, one billionaire's son, one police lieutenant, and one criminal lawyer had been given their orders. What could possibly go wrong? Alexander had it all planned, didn't he? He had done his job perfectly and if we did ours as perfectly, the alleged perpetrator was as good as in jail right now.

Let's see: half a ballet troupe without sets and without an orchestra; one empty theater with all the lights out; six suspects, one of whom is the killer who is going to try to kill my husband; one altered costume; one court steno; one police lieutenant with two plainclothesmen; two video camera/recorders; one spotlight; one choreographer with a sense of humor playing a crooked ballet critic; one forger; one conceited genius detective in a wheelchair, recreating the crime whereby the guy in the wheelchair gets himself killed; and one idiot wife, with orders not to interfere.

And a bullhorn.

This wasn't going to be a ballet, it was going to be a circus. A Russian circus. All that was missing was a magic flute. And a whip.

24

I had cut off the bell on Alexander's extension to let him sleep undisturbed, so, a half hour later, I was the one who had to argue with Evan Spenser.

"Mrs. Gold," he said, "if you won't let me talk to Mr. Gold, at least transmit my objections to him."

"No," I said firmly into the phone, "this is what he wants and you have to cooperate."

"But—, but—" he sputtered, "if it isn't Jeffrey, why doesn't he just tell the police who it is?"

"Why don't you conduct with a salami instead of a baton, Mr. Spenser? Because that's how Alexander wants to do it, and that's how it's going to be done. Or else."

"Or else what?" he shouted. "This is ridiculous. I'm not going to do it."

"That," I told him, "is the best way to make Max Baron angry and to cancel the Russian tour. Is that what you want?"

"I talk with her," I could hear Zoris Ziladiev say in the background. After a moment he came on the phone. "Madame," he asked, "why you do this? Is crazy stupid, you know."

"Please, Mr. Ziladiev," I said. "Please cooperate. Don't you want the killer caught?"

"Better no," he answered immediately. "If not Jeffrey, must be member of company. You want put in jail, wait after Russian tour."

"Mr. Ziladiev, if you don't put on the ballet this evening, there will be *no* Russian tour. Don't you understand that?"

There was a moment's silence, then, "I understand. Is always the boss, the commissar, the money, not the artist. You know how bad is now? All my little girls very nervous; my boys more. Not know yes or no. Not know if get pay or no. Pack, unpack, pack again. Lose costume, lose prop. Mix up. Spoil tour. You want this?"

"I am sure," I said fatuously, "that you will handle everything well, right after Alexander catches the killer."

"How catch killer? You crazy? You think killer make same as with Boguslav? Try kill Gold, police catch? No. Only stupid killer do. You say do same as when Boguslav is kill. Hah! If I killer, what you think I do? I stay in dressing room, what I do. Nothing, I do. So how catch?"

"Mr. Gold is never wrong." I wish I believed that. "He knows the killer must reveal himself."

"If Gold think killer is stupid, do not make performance. Only one stupid in company: Kurt Tindall. Tell police. Is better we go without Tindall."

"The police can't just arrest Tindall. They need evidence."

"So? Is easy. Put Tindall in room with big policeman. Say, 'You not confess, I hit face.' In one minute, he confess."

"Mr. Ziladiev," I begged, "please don't waste time. Go do what must be done, and quickly. Make Spenser cooperate. If everything is not exactly the way Alexander said, there will be no tour. Do you understand that? NO TOUR!"

I hung up, feeling even worse than before. Ziladiev was right. Only an idiot would attack Alexander in the box. All the killer had to do was nothing, and Alexander would be in the same position as before. Unless there was a way

Alexander could make the killer reveal himself. If there was, I sure didn't see it.

Just as I had settled down again, the doorbell rang. It was Tatiana Kusnitzova, very boiling angry. She started in without even taking off her coat. "What the hell are you trying to do? Do you have any idea what is involved in preparing a performance? Or in packing it up for an overseas tour?"

I had had it with everyone yelling at me. "Sweetie," I said, "don't worry about packing again. The tour is out. All I have to do is call Lieutenant Warshafsky and tell him that Alexander has pulled off the case. The police will keep you here forever."

She paled and sat down on the couch. I twisted the knife. "Everybody is telling me how hard it is to put on this performance. Bull! It's no harder than a one-night stand in the provinces. Easier. No orchestra, no stage preparation, no lights, one lousy ballet instead of three. You know what I think? I think you're all afraid to upset the apple cart; that you all know one of you did it, not Jeffrey, and don't want the real killer exposed."

She looked up at me, suddenly small and drawn, looking ten years older than her age. "No, Mrs. Gold, I guess we don't want the killer exposed, not really, if it isn't Jeffrey. But it is Jeffrey, too, isn't it? Anyone in the company could have done it, with Jeffrey's help. The trouble is, you don't want to accept that; that's why we're going through this charade. And it *is* a lot of trouble, unnecessary trouble, at the worst possible time."

"Why don't you tell me who did it, then? And how? If it fits, we'll call off the show."

"Why don't you ask Jeffrey, if you really want to know. Have you really pressed him? Or do billionaires' sons get treated better than dancers?"

"In this world, Tatiana, in any world, the powerful get

treated better than the weak. But we did press Jeffrey," I said, remembering the time I gave him, "and he didn't confess. Also, my husband says, knows, Jeffrey is innocent, and he's never wrong." Well, hardly ever, I said to myself.

"I see I can't make you change your mind," she said. "But tell me, how will this performance accomplish anything?"

I couldn't answer that; no way. So I said, almost truthfully, "I won't tell you that, it would spoil the plan. But I can tell you that you are a prime suspect. You want to make things easy? Confess now, and let the show go on."

She stood up and smiled contemptuously. "You don't know a thing and you can't prove a thing. You want to play games? Have fun." She whirled out, opening the doors herself.

I debated waking Alexander, but decided I could tell him later, since I could detect nothing in these interchanges that could be of any use to him.

There was one thing, though. Ziladiev's suggestion. If all else failed, put each suspect in a bare soundproofed room with a big policeman. Or an angry wife, with a sick husband and a million dollars at stake. Me.

25

I had set the little bell attached to the latch of the Boguslav box carefully, not hanging down, but balanced precariously on top of the chair back so that the slightest movement of the latch would warn Alexander that someone was trying to sneak into his box. And warn me, via the monitor.

As I climbed through the curtain into the Barons' box, I thought that I should have done the same for that box too —the dark corridor outside made it too easy for a killer— but that way lay madness. What would stop the killer from entering the next box over and climbing over the short divider—or two, or three—or four? Besides, I had brought only one bell.

Alexander was alone, in a wheelchair, in exactly the same position Boguslav had been when he was killed.

I could see clearly enough from the right-of-center box, sitting low and motionless so that the faint glow from the stage lights would not give away my presence. The video monitors were turned low too, so that their sound could be heard only by those who were in the box. The center box being full of spotlight and video camera, we had all moved right one box: Pearl, Burton and I, Warshafsky and the steno, and the two TV monitors.

The theater was almost completely dark, with only the tops of the seat backs tipped by the faint light. Everything was ready, the house curtain framing the stage as it had on the gala night, the head down about ten feet, the wings six feet in. The video cameras were aimed and focussed, two men running the audio system for the ballet music, two more on the stage lighting and the controls, and one on the spotlight. Warshafsky's men were nowhere to be seen; keeping an eye on the dark corridor, I hoped. The six suspects were in the places they had claimed to be and the dancers were in the wings all dressed up and made up, waiting. A miracle of organization it was, except that it was 7:00 PM, fifteen minutes behind schedule.

"Ready to start," Alexander said through the bullhorn. The dancers formed a group on the stage. "Start the music," Alexander said. There was a great snap of plucked strings, the percussion pounded, and the dance began. Without the brilliant lighting, everything seemed less intense, less surprising, slower. The dancers moved outward from their clump, expanding like a flower. Hurkos appeared in center stage on the rising piston, and the whirling atom dance began. They danced faster and faster until the great discord sounded, then the great bang of tympany, and the scene was over.

And no one had tried to kill Alexander.

On the lighted stage I saw how the dancers had been able to find their way in the total darkness of the premiere production. There were stanchions lined up, holding lines of light rope, which guided them to their beginning spots. The music was downstage to orient the dancers, and their own marvelous sense of place and direction did the rest. I think they could have performed in total darkness, as Alicia Alonso effectively did by dancing when she was almost totally blind.

The dancers, each helped by a dresser waiting at a fixed position, were now in their furred warrior costumes. They quickly assembled themselves into the rectangular array and began dancing to the beat of the kettledrum, Pierre leading the group.

Hurkos slowly walked into position and when he raised his hands, the group of men began their military march pattern. They came together around Hurkos, handed him the gold handles of their belts, and formed the huge human wheel. The wheel began turning and pulsing, and I marvelled again at Danilo's strength and the precision of the dancers. The great discord sounded again, the extraordinary jumping turn that wrapped the belt around each dancer, and the scene ended. The male dancers started walking slowly toward the lines at the back of the stage, buckling their belts. The women went all the way back into the wings. Hurkos walked to his line, moved along it toward center stage, came to the end, and took two measured paces more, and faced front, ready for the jumping line scene.

The music started again, and the first man took his place in front of Hurkos, knees slightly bent, waiting for the musical cue. The drumbeat sounded, the man jumped, and Alexander yelled, "Cut!"

Everything stopped dead. All eyes turned toward Alexander's box. "Will you please rewind the music tape to just before the end of the last scene," he said. "And all dancers take the places they were in just after the Ba'aal released the belts and after they were wrapped around you. Belts unbuckled, please." Alexander was standing up in the front of the box, looking at the circle of dancers on the stage.

"Hurkos," Alexander said, "please close your eyes, make believe you're in total darkness, just as in the performance, and move slowly into your position for the jumping line scene." Hurkos did an about face, walked upstage to the line with careful paces, found the stanchion, and followed the line to the right. At the end of the line, he took his two paces, faced front, and waited.

"Now, the first jumper," Alexander announced, "please close your eyes and take your position." A dancer from the rear of the circle walked to the guideline and moved along the line until he was only a step away from Hurkos.

"Now, the second man, please," Alexander said. Another dancer moved into position, one pace behind the first.

"Next—, next—, next—" Alexander called out, until thirteen dancers were lined up, ready to start the scene.

"Now Mr. Romanoff." Pierre started moving back. Alexander stopped him. "No, no, go back to where you were, center stage front." Pierre went back.

"Please close your eyes, Mr. Romanoff." Alexander said through the bullhorn, "Turn ninety degrees right, put your hands out sideways, and walk until you touch the edge of the curtain." Pierre did so. He was now right in front of Alexander's box. "Turn left and face me, Mr. Romanoff; you can open your eyes."

Alexander turned to the back of the theater. "Please turn the spotlight on Mr. Romanoff," he ordered. Pierre flinched slightly at the sudden brilliance, then resumed his graceful stance. "Now, Mr. Romanoff, unwind the belt from your waist and throw the end up to me." Pierre hesitated for a moment, then unwound the belt and threw it underhand toward Alexander. It fell far short.

"I'm sorry, Mr. Romanoff, I forgot. Pull back the belt. Take off your heavy fur hat, put the chin strap through the belt buckle and loop it over so it holds. Now throw the hat up to me." Pierre looked around and seemed to see no alternative. He swung the weighted belt once and let it go. It made a graceful curve and landed right in Alexander's wheelchair.

"Thank you," Alexander said, and took off his jacket. He was wearing his wide heavy weightlifting belt. He turned so that he faced the video camera focussed on his box and said quietly, "This is for the record." He had lashed two of my screw-in clothes hooks to the wide belt, the long side against the belt, the short curved hooks protruding. He placed the straight side of the D-shaped buckle of Pierre's belt in the outstanding hooks. "Now, Warshafsky, tell the man you have at the dressing rooms to have Zoris, Kurt, and Betsy come to the box where you are. Also the man you have at the back of the orchestra to do the same with Spenser and Tatiana. Then have both your men take their positions." Warshafsky quietly relayed these instructions on his walkie-talkie.

Alexander turned back to face the stage. "Okay, Pierre," he said, "I have you hooked securely on my belt. Please climb up here." Pierre suddenly got angry. "This is enough. There will be no more the foolishness." He stepped forward to slacken the belt and moved to release the clamp that held the belt around his waist. At once, Alexander pulled the belt tight again. Pierre stepped forward again and Alexander tightened the belt again, like a fisherman playing a trout. One more step and Pierre was at the edge of the stage. Alexander pulled again, and Pierre was overbalanced. He tried to straighten up, but it was too late; he fell off the stage toward the orchestra pit. Alexander quickly pulled the belt in, and Pierre was hanging, dangling, held by the belt, swinging back and forth, out into the darkness and back into the spotlight, swinging slowly, slowly, in the bright cone.

Alexander held the belt with Pierre on it easily with one hand. With the other he raised the bullhorn and announced, "That's it, everybody. Costumes off. Pack up everything and go to the airport. You're all going to Russia." The stage emptied rapidly.

Just then, Spenser entered the box, followed a moment later by Tatiana. I motioned them to stay in the rear cloakroom area of the box. Spenser nodded toward the monitor and said to Tatiana, "Pierre. Who would have believed it?" "I would," she answered cooly, "and so would any woman. But I thought he would just explode one day; I never believed he would plan it."

Ziladiev, dressed as the Charlatan, came in, rapidly. He looked relieved when he saw Spenser. "So, it is not you, Evan? Good."

"I was concerned that it might have been you, old man," Spenser answered, and put his arm around Ziladiev.

Tindall, in his Moor's costume, came in. His eye caught the monitors. "See? It *was* Pierre. I always said it was him, but nobody believed me. Ugly old dwarf."

Ziladiev turned on Kurt. "You. Shut up stupid mouth or I kill you dead myself now. You hear? You never be dancer as Pierre. Or man. Never." Kurt shrank into the corner.

Betsy, dressed as the Ballerina, came in slowly, as if afraid of what she might find. She looked at the others, then at the monitor, and broke down completely, sobbing, as though the pressures of the last few days, of her whole life, had suddenly burst loose. Tatiana hesitated, then put her arms around the little girl, carefully avoiding Betsy's made-up face. Betsy leaned on Tatiana, and with a what-the-hell shrug, Tatiana held her close, smearing Betsy's makeup over her beautiful gray tweed suit.

I whispered, "Everyone keep quiet or I'll throw you all out." Their eyes turned to the monitor.

Pierre was raging, screaming at Alexander in French too fast for me to follow. Alexander calmly said, "Climb up, Pierre, you look foolish hanging there. No sense pretending you can't do it." Pierre cursed him louder. Alexander kept urging him to climb up. Suddenly, as if making a decision, Pierre reached up and climbed hand over hand, like a monkey, fast, up the belt and into the box.

I turned to the second monitor to watch the murder box at close range.

Alexander sat, half reclining, in the wheelchair, outstretched feet against the end wall of the box, with Pierre standing at his left. The plaited belt was slack, and Pierre slowly and calmly, with his lips pressed tightly together, pushed the parts of the clasp together and loosened the belt so that it fell from his waist to the floor. He then leaned over Alexander and unhooked the big buckle from the hooks on Alexander's belt.

Still holding the buckle, he said in a tightly controlled voice, "You think to humiliate me, sir? You think I am the puppet to hang by the string for my colleagues to make laugh? You think is the joke? I am tired of the joke, sir, and now there will be no more." With that he jumped, with amazing speed, behind the wheelchair, wrapped the belt around Alexander's neck, and began to strangle him.

26

Instinctively I grabbed my big bag to dash to the front box to kill Romanoff. But I remembered Alexander's insistence that I must not interefere, no matter what. Warshafsky had drawn his gun and was looking helplessly for a position to shoot from where the box's curtain would not block his view. "Don't worry," I told him inanely. "Look at the monitor."

As long as Romanoff didn't have a knife, I felt sure that Alexander could handle it. In fact, this was probably the first time in his life that he battled a man shorter than he is. Fit as Romanoff was, Alexander was a powerlifter, one of the strongest men in New York. On the other hand, Alexander had not yet fully recovered from his heart attack and had not been in a gym for three months.

Leaning back in a wheelchair with a belt tight around your neck is not the best position to work from. Alexander twisted hard to his left and the chair with the two men crashed to the floor. Alexander got on his hands and knees, Romanoff still twisting the garrote tight, and slowly stood up. Romanoff tried to lean back, to get his feet on the ground, but to Alexander, one hundred and twenty pounds is nothing. He put his hands behind his neck, grasped each of Romanoff's wrists, and slowly pulled them apart.

Still holding Romanoff's wrists in his powerful grip, Alexander bent forward quickly and flipped Romanoff over his head, taking care to let the dancer land on his feet. Without letting go, Alexander passed his right hand over Romanoff's head, turning him around to face Alexander, helpless. Alexander backed him into the front corner of the box and said, "I have every right to break your back, but I want to talk to you. Sit down." Alexander released him, righted the wheelchair, and sat Romanoff down in it. Reaching through the curtain, Alexander pulled out a chair and sat down facing the still-defiant dancer.

They stared at each other for a moment, then Alexander spoke. "You fought the Nazis in Paris when you were ten years old, you and your older sister. That was brave. You must have been couriers for the Resistance."

Pierre did not answer for a while, then said in a resigned

voice, "They did not permit young boys to have the guns. Small boys and young girls carried messages and small—items to the men and women who fought. I was small for my age. Usually the Nazis did not check us."

"But when they did? Under torture, anyone will break, Pierre. Especially a child. The Resistance taught these couriers a simple trick, a possible way to avoid torture."

"To run away, melt away, in an alley. We knew the Metro, the streets, the stores."

"But if you were cornered? How could a young woman or a small boy avoid capture, Pierre? Simple. By killing the Nazi. There was a special trick for this. A small knife, in the left hand. Step close to the Nazi instead of pulling away. Insert the knife under the tip of the breastbone and push upward to the right. It penetrates the heart easily at exactly the right angle: forty-five degrees in and forty-five degrees up to the right. The natural motion."

Pierre was silent, staring at the floor. Alexander continued. "Boguslav was lying tilted back on his wheelchair; the position he assumed so he could anchor your climb up to the box, your buckle hooked onto his longhorn buckle. You were standing on his left, where you would have to be after climbing up to the box. The little knife was in the scabbard of the fake sword on your right hip, kept from falling deep into the scabbard by the loop of nylon around the sword hilt. You pulled out the front of Boguslav's blouse with your left hand. Why he let you do it, we'll go into later. And who but you could have known that Jeffrey would be confined to the cloak area? Would anyone else have risked killing Viktor with Jeffrey in the box? Impossible."

Pierre rubbed his face with both hands, streaking his makeup, the downward lines of his fingers making him look like a clown crying. Alexander waited until Pierre dropped his hands and went on. "You placed your left hand under the pulled-up blouse, laid the knife, still held by its nylon loop to avoid fingerprints, on the blouse in your left hand. Which way the knife faced was unimportant; both edges were sharpened. Your right hand covered Boguslav's mouth and nose while your left hand slid the knife, at the appropriate angle, under his breastbone into his heart. To make doubly sure, you sliced it back and forth several times and, at the end, pushed it all the way in. Although Boguslav was three times as big as you, the surprise, and his weakness—he could no longer even dress himself—made the killing easy."

The spotlight operator, faithful to his orders, still had the spot on Pierre. The ten of us in the center box, were clustered around the monitor, unable to move. Pierre had a fixed smile on his face, like the sad, crooked smile he wore when he was Petrouchka. "You think I must to say something?" he asked. "You have the microphone here to record? You are the fool, Mr. Gold."

Alexander went on lecturing, quietly. "Almost from the day you met, he was unfaithful. He betrayed you again and again. You were true, you wanted nothing but love, tranquillity, a home. And to dance. He wanted excitement, challenge, battle even. He had to outwit, to outfight, dominate, fool people; to trick them and to make them like it. All, everyone, was to be used to make the Boguslav Ballet Russe the greatest company in the world. And to substitute, not sublimate, but substitute, for his inability to be a dancer himself."

"It was not so important," said Pierre, a little bitterly I thought, "that he was unfaithful. The others meant nothing; he always came home."

"He was a cruel man, Pierre. He manipulated people for the pleasure of it. As he manipulated you, even you. Why did he want you to climb up here in the two minutes—"

Pierre raised his hand to stop Alexander, then dropped it resignedly. "It was not to talk business, was it Pierre? Or to discuss what you would cook for supper tomorrow. No, it had to be another of his manipulations, tricks, so-called practical jokes, the ones with his own little twists in them that ended up with someone in pain, or hurt, or humiliated. What was it, Pierre?"

Pierre looked at Alexander sadly, the crooked smile painted on his face; not speaking; dumb.

"You had three minutes, Pierre, even though the blackout was supposed to be only a little over a minute. The tape that we played, I timed it, gives one minute twenty seconds. There was long heavy applause at the end of the turning wheel scene; it held up the start of the next scene, the jumping line scene, for a little longer than the composer intended. But there were also thirteen dancers ahead of you in that scene, and the only ones visible were in the spotlight. Each dancer had to make three jumps and take a step; close to five seconds per man, before you had to appear on stage. Total time, over three minutes. Climbing up here, getting down, going to your position—you had the spotlight to guide you now, you could go directly to your position without using the guidelines—say thirty seconds. What did you do here, or rather, what were you going to do that might be done in two and one-half minutes."

Pierre looked at Alexander, his arms in the stiff, clumsy attitude of the doll, Petrouchka, begging for the knowledge that would kill him.

"And the new curtain between Boguslav's box and the next box—what was it for? He had never done anything like that before. Privacy? Boguslav, the publicity hound, wanted privacy? To do what?"

Petrouchka stared straight ahead.

"There's a clue you don't know about, Pierre. In his last

letter to the teacher in Austin, he told her he wanted to have his letters published, unexpurgated. He wrote that he was going to play his last joke; one for the record books, he put it. And he didn't scream when you pulled out his blouse. What did he threaten you with, Pierre? What did he promise you, to induce you to indulge him in this fantastic sexual encounter? And with Jeffrey only four feet away to heighten the thrill. A quickie, consummated during the supposed one-minute blackout in front of two thousand people; that's how it would go down in the record books. No one would easily break that record. Or figure out that there were really three minutes. You would be famous, Pierre. Not for your dancing, of course; people would soon forget that, they would only remember your name as the One-Minute-Wonder. Is that how you really want to be remembered, Pierre? You couldn't even fake sickness; Viktor knew you could not miss your Farewell Performance."

Pierre now had his head bent all the way to one side, in the classic Petrouchka pose made famous by Nijinsky. He stared into nowhere. Or into the hell of the inarticulate.

"Of course, what he promised you was that he would give you a written contract to become general manager and artistic director after the Russian tour. But you knew that was a lie. You had already found a copy of the contract he had signed for Tatiana, absolutely binding, prepared by a lawyer. No doubt you checked it with a lawyer yourself." Alexander leaned forward and stared at Pierre intently. He looked as though he felt as sick about what he was doing as I did.

"What else did he lie to you about, Pierre? Were you absolutely sure he would let you climb down the belt, swing over the stage, and then unhook the buckle from his belt? Suppose he left you swinging there until the scene ended and the lights went up? It would only be another minute, and it would be positive proof that he had accomplished his record. You would be left exposed, hanging, like a fool, like a puppet, strings held by the Charlatan, for everyone to see. It would be just like him; he's done worse things in the past. He might find it funny; you would find it, at best, unprofessional. And you would have to leave the ballet world. Not just this company, but all dance. Who could work under you after this? Could such a laughing stock be *régisseur*, even for a tiny local group? You would die without the ballet. So, even though you really did not want to, he forced you to kill him."

Petrouchka knew, with absolute certainty, that the Charlatan had never intended to let him live.

"Did he also tell you it was his last wish? His dying wish? That you owed it to him for all he did for you? That without him you would still be a *caractère*? Did he bring in this lie too, to play on your sympathies?"

Petrouchka knew he must die soon; the music was signaling the end of the show.

"And if you refused, Pierre? As you no doubt did. He would not let you. Even if it did not happen, he would say it had. He had done this before; you knew that. Denials would not help; would only make things worse. It would be the same, whether you did or not. You had no choice. Except one. And he was dying anyway; would be dead in a month or two anyway. So it was not really murder, Pierre, it was an act of mercy for someone you once loved."

Pierre straightened up, his eyes burning, catching the light from the spot, reflecting the light like an animal's eyes. "This is all in the mind, Mr. Gold. Conjecture. There is not the proof."

"Sure there is, Pierre. There are fibers from the rug on your pants, fibers from the velvet-covered railing on your clothes, marks on your belt buckle from the horns on Boguslav's belt."

"They all come from now, when I was forced by you to climb up."

"No, Pierre. The costume you wore for the premiere of *Graven Image* is in the police laboratory right now, being checked. We had a new costume made for you for tonight. You may have put the stiffness to the cleaning, but it's the newness. And the knife sharpener in your kitchen, the stone has particles of the steel of the murder knife in it."

Pierre folded his hands across his chest, stubbornly. "No one will believe this story; it is too fantastic."

Alexander nodded. "You may be right, Pierre; that is why you are going to confess. There is certainly enough evidence to try you, but it is possible that you may not be convicted. And considering that you were ready to allow Jeffrey to go to jail, you deserve to be convicted. So, if you do not confess, plead guilty, it will be necessary to read this at the trial. To show motive. I hope that you will agree that it is better for you that this letter is not made public."

Alexander took a single sheet of notepaper out of his pocket, unfolded it, and said, "This is addressed to the board of directors of the Boguslav Ballet Russe." Alexander held the letter up to the light of the spot and began reading:

I am pleased that you have accepted my decision that Tatiana Kusnitzova is to take my place next season as General Manager and Artistic Director.

With respect to Pierre Romanoff, I regret that no place can be found for him in this company. His lack of administrative ability makes it impossible to find some sort of desk job for him, and there is no question of his replacing Zoris

Ziladiev. Naturally, I will exert every effort to place him in some small regional company where his remaining talents may still be of some use.

Because of my past personal relationship with Mr. Romanoff, I had kept him on as *premier dan-seur* far beyond the time he should have been retired, forcibly, if necessary. I regret this mistake, especially as this almost cost us the services of Kurt Tindall, a truly remarkable dancer who will soon, I predict, make the world forget Nijinsky.

It has been painful for me to watch Romanoff, once one of the best dancers, deteriorate to the point where I had to beg the critics not to write of his failings. In the past season I have seen him, many times, hunching his shoulders, not maintaining a clean position, landing clumsily and not facing in the right direction. Once he almost fell over. In a *tour en l'air* he does not start or end in good fifth position, he does not point his feet, and they are often separated and not well turned out. I could go on and on. His *élévation,* of course, is very poor, and with Tindall on the stage, poor Romanoff looks like an amateur. Then too . . .''

Pierre jumped up and snatched the letter from Alexander's hands. "This is the lie. It is the forgery; it was not written by Viktor. Viktor could not write this of me. I dance with perfection." He held the letter up to the spotlight.

"Isn't that Viktor's notepaper?" Alexander asked. "Is not that his handwriting; his signature?"

"It cannot be," Pierre said in fury. He looked like the vengeful ghost of Petrouchka in the last scene. "It is the false writing." He stuffed the letter into his vest and started to walk through the curtain of the box. "You will not show this."

Alexander shifted his chair to block him. Pierre stepped back, turned to his left and crouched slightly. Alexander quickly crossed his hands in front of his chest and face, then slowly dropped his hands, leaving himself unprotected. "No savate, Pierre, please. I have just recovered from a severe heart attack. One kick could kill me."

Pierre hesitated, still crouching, his right foot held ready to kick out, to get Alexander out of the way so he could escape to the corridor. Alexander faced him calmly. I wondered why Alexander was taking this chance; what he had to gain from it? Pierre had killed before, why shouldn't he kill again? I was too far away to do anything; I could only wait. I knew Alexander was fast, but was he, at forty-nine, fast enough and strong enough to block a savate kick from a trained dancer?

With a cry of rage, Pierre turned around, climbed over the low railing and kicked off from the end wall of the box toward the stage. We all gasped, and I could visualize his body broken in half over the sharp back of a seat below. But I had forgotten that the stage curtain was open about six feet, and was only eight feet from the end of the box.

Pierre flew across the eight feet like a diver and hit the huge heavy stage curtain perfectly. In two seconds he slid down gently to the stage, landing without a sound. Just before he landed the two big plainclothesmen, who had evidently been waiting there, stepped out from behind the curtain. Each grabbed one of Pierre's arms.

Pierre went crazy, screaming and fighting with such fury that the two big men were thrown back and forth for several seconds. But size and strength told, and Pierre was held motionless between them, in the spotlight, his back to the audience. Then slowly, slowly, he collapsed in a pile of sawdust, not a dry eye in the house as we watched the life ebb from the empty shell.

They always said that Pierre Romanoff could tear your heart out with a single gesture.

27

"What has happened to Roberta?" Julia Baron asked, working two crepe pans at once. "She is never late."

It was Monday night. We were all, Susan, Jeffrey and Max Baron, Pearl and Burton, Alexander and I, sitting in Julia Baron's favorite meeting place, around the kitchen table. She was making *chremzl,* the wonderfully light *mehlspeise* made of separated eggs, cottage cheese, flour, sugar, and vanilla, just so we wouldn't starve to death by nine o'clock.

"And what's keeping Warshafsky?" Alexander asked. "I told him 8:30. If he doesn't come in five minutes, I'm going to start without him."

"Start now," Max Baron said. "I do not think he is as interested in your thought processes as in evidence he can present to a court of law."

"Sure," Alexander said, leaning back in his chair and clearing his throat. "If anyone had come in through the door of the box, Jeffrey would have known about it. Granted that Betsy and Tatiana could have squeezed through easily, but not without waking Jeffrey, so it's highly improbable. Then for either of them to have left the same way multiplies the improbability. Neither of them could have known that Jeffrey would be in the cloakroom. The killer, finding the door blocked, would most likely have gone away to try another time. The motives were such, and the opportunities, that a day or a week later would not have mattered. Who but Pierre was under time pressure?

"Add to that the other clues: the blouse tucked in to expose the longhorn buckle; the pulled-out blouse; the tilted back of the wheelchair; the handleless knife with the nylon loop. Nothing fitted. If Jeffrey did it, or was an accomplice, what was the meaning of these clues? To throw off the police? But then, Boguslav himself ordered that he be dressed with the blouse tucked in. The killer could not have known about that, unless the killer were Jeffrey and/or Pierre. So the most likely assumption was that Jeffrey was not involved in the crime."

"You're leaving out Boguslav's psychology," said Pearl. "That was very important."

"Of course," said Alexander. "He changed his name and started a new life. Why that name? Viktor, in Russian, means the same as it does in English: winner, conqueror, although it is archaic in Russian. Today the word used in Russian is *pobedatel,* as near as I can say it. But Viktor represented what Boguslav wanted to be. In all his past, every time someone did him wrong, he got his revenge, usually by means of a practical joke with a very painful sting in the end. This pattern developed in Boguslav to the point where it became an end in itself, where he would perpetrate his jokes for the pleasure of the joke, such as it was, even to the point of causing pain in those he worked with, depended on, or even loved. Pierre and Jeffrey, to name only two."

"I never thought of it before," said Max Baron, "but Boguslav has a meaning in Russian, too."

"Yes," said Alexander, "it means, roughly, 'one who serves a god.' And it was a fitting name, since Viktor Boguslav gave his life to the service of Terpsichore, of ballet. But at the time he took that name, I doubt that he knew enough Russian to choose it for that reason. In English it has another meaning: 'bogus-Slav,' which fits what we know of the man quite well. If he ever found out the Russian meaning, he would have enjoyed the play on words immensely."

"Didn't his English names have a meaning too?" asked Mrs. Baron. "In German?"

"All three," Alexander agreed. "Caspar is the American version of 'Kasper,' the German puppet hero of the *Kasperletheater,* or Punch and Judy show. Beaufort means beautiful and strong. Smith is a worker in hot metal. So the puppet became the conqueror, the worker in hot metal became the servant of the dance who worked in sweating bodies, and instead of hitting other puppets on the head with a club, the Charlatan hit them with a whip, literally and figuratively. I'm sure he found it funny."

"Is that why he put on *Graven Image?*" Burton asked. "For a joke?"

"It fits the pattern. It was not only so he could have another role on the stage, although I think he would have given his life to dance once, just once, as well as Pierre Romanoff did."

"But I thought he didn't like the way Pierre danced any more," Pearl said. "In the letter to the board . . ."

Alexander said, "I wrote it, Boguslav style. The forger, remember? Anyway, when Viktor first conceived the idea of *Graven Image,* he was only looking for a vehicle in which he could have the starring role. Note that there was no one else on the stage with any real identity; even Pierre, as the Leader, was practically invisible and nameless. But as the idea grew, he decided to make it a modern ballet, to shock everyone, from the audience to his colleagues to the board of directors. Then he commissioned a new ballet with new music, spending money that could have been used to pay his employees and colleagues, in effect taking it out of their pockets and making them pay for their own humiliation; one of his favorite themes. Then he brought in an outside composer, Juspada, to annoy Spenser, and an outside choreographer, Augustine, to annoy Ziladiev. Finally, he put Pierre in a less important role than his own."

"Don't forget Tatiana," I reminded. "He got her too."

"I didn't forget her," he said, "and neither did Boguslav. *Gala Performance* was his needle into her hide for making him sign her contract. And bringing in the Russian defector, Boruskaya, and the Ballet Theater star, Trebshinska, made it even worse. And he didn't let Betsy Gilman dance in it at all, to show her that to him she wasn't a star."

"And Pierre, in *Petrouchka,*" said Pearl. "He had Pierre killed by Kurt Tindall in the ballet to emphasize that Tindall was replacing Pierre professionally."

"Exactly," Alexander said. "So he decided to play all his games in one final fling, to give a Gala Performance of his own, in which all his colleagues would be tortured or humiliated, including Jeffrey; in which he would play out a joke for the record books, one which would be made public shortly after his death, and which would destroy his friend and lover of twenty years."

"Was he really going to leave Pierre hanging there?" Pearl asked. "Would he have ruined the ballet just for that?"

"Why not?" Alexander said. "That way he could have hurt Juspada and Augustine too. Pierre evidently believed he would."

"He was a monster," said Julia Baron. "I hope that Pierre is set free."

"If you will retain America's most expensive criminal lawyer . . ." I said, smiling.

"It has already been arranged," Max Baron replied.

"So," said Alexander, impatient at the interruption, "we have the exposed longhorn belt buckle. Why exposed? Was he going to gore somebody? In his box? No. Combined with the tilted-back wheelchair and his insistence on being placed exactly in the corner with the footrest tight against the end wall, it could only have been for Boguslav to be an anchor. Well, once I understood that the killer had not come from the corridor, and had to have come from the stage, it had to be a rope or rope ladder or—it was right there in front of me, a belt."

"So why the trip to the library?" I asked.

"For the unusual stab wound. If the killer climbed up the belt—Pierre, who else could it be?—he had to stand on Boguslav's left. That meant that the knife was in his left hand striking underhand. I had a feeling I had read about this before, and I had. It was a method taught to many Resistance couriers, kids who couldn't fight a Nazi in other ways."

"And the shirt pulled out led to the idea of sex?" asked Burton.

"Precisely. Why else would Boguslav have allowed his blouse to be pulled out in silence? And what was to have been his big joke for the record books?"

"With Jeffrey on the other side of the curtain?" Pearl asked.

"I'm sure Boguslav intended to tell him all about it the next day. In detail. As additional humiliation."

"Well," said Max Baron, "that was a truly brilliant job under very difficult conditions. I congratulate you, Mr. Gold. I wish you would reconsider working with me."

"How about right now, Mr. Baron?" Alexander said. "You

were going to retain me to solve a business problem, remember? You wanted to find out how and by whom your mind was being read. Do you still want me to do it?"

"Certainly, Mr. Gold. As soon as possible, please. The terms you have already discussed with Burton."

"Tax free, Mr. Baron. If you please. After the million you gave me before, I'm in a very high tax bracket this year."

Baron smiled ruefully. "Very well, then, tax free. But I too place a limit. Thirty days. After that, you turn all information over to me for nothing. From right now. And you must also show me how to stop it."

"Agreed then, Mr. Baron." Alexander smiled. "We have a meeting of the minds and a contract. And I don't need the thirty days."

"Now?" Baron looked at him in amazement. "You mean right now?"

"Now. Let's start with this. You have allowed a fraud to be perpetrated by your public relations people. You do not always make the correct decision. Your wife does. Ever since you met her, she has made all the important decisions, saved both your lives many times, and made it possible for you to build an empire."

Julia Baron placed her hand on her husband's shoulder, quieting him so she could speak first. "That is not true, Mr. Gold," she said. "Max and I, we are one. We discuss things together, certainly, as a husband and wife do. Then Max does what he thinks is right. And he is always right."

Baron smiled at his wife. "It is too late, Julia, and Mr. Gold is too observant." He turned toward Alexander. "Yes, it is true. And I do not mind that it is known now. Julia has the ability and I have the absolute trust in her. Also, I am a very good administrator."

"You didn't listen to her one time," Alexander reminded.

"You mean when I helped Jeffrey to get the position with

Boguslav? Yes, that was a mistake. And I paid for it. One million dollars. Tax free. But what if my wife is always right? She knows little of my business."

"She is a pattern maker," Alexander said, "as I am. All she needs is a few points and she unconsciously fills in the rest. And she has an advantage over me: She is always right."

"So how does her knowledge get to the Street?"

"She talked to Jeffrey about many things, probably tried to encourage him in business, told him what his future could be, should be, in your operations."

"I never told him anything specific," Julia Baron said.

"You didn't have to," Alexander answered. "Jeffrey, trying to make himself important, trying to impress Boguslav, told his boss what he remembered. Boguslav made his stock purchases on these projections. Boguslav's broker, seeing he had a client who seemed to have accurate inside information, touted all his clients onto these same stocks. Ergo, a minor ripple was created in the market, which you were acute enough to catch. It seemed to you that someone knew your mind. Presto, it is now over."

"Mr. Gold," Baron said, "you have tricked me into a no-lose bet."

"No tricks," Alexander said. "I gave you what I promised and what you wanted. What would it have cost you if you had to act, for only the next year, as though the Street knew what you were thinking? You got away cheap."

"Now I'm to blame for Dad losing money," said Jeffrey bitterly. "It's always like that. In the company they were all jealous. There was no reason to make Spenser acting general manager. And even if they did, why couldn't he have taken me to Russia as his assistant? I got things done."

"Spenser was chosen, and I concurred, because he is level-headed and conservative, and will do nothing badly," said

Max Baron. "And if anything does go wrong in Russia, it will not count against Tatiana, who will make an excellent general manager next season. And there was a very good reason why he did not pick you for his personal assistant: Spenser's little harpist is prettier than you. You must learn that life affects business decisions, if you are to become a good businessman."

"Then what am I going to do?" Jeffrey asked.

"I suggest that you find a job where you can learn and grow, and possibly be happy and productive," his father said.

"Okay, Dad," Jeffrey said. "Which one of your companies . . .?"

"I think," his mother interrupted, "that you would be better off in a strange company."

Just then Roberta and Lieutenant Warshafsky walked in together. I don't mean at the same time, I mean *together*. Looking at them I knew now who Warshafsky's possible Sunday morning date was. Roberta was glowing and even Warshafsky's rough face seemed relaxed.

Warshafsky sat down at the table to talk with the others. Roberta kissed her father, then motioned me to join her and her mother at the stove. She put her arms around her mother and whispered, "I think I am going to marry David."

"But Roberta," her mother said, "you've only known each other for—what?—four days? Are you sure?"

"How long did you know Father before you were sure?" Roberta asked.

"Four seconds," Julia Baron said. "But the situation was different. Are you sure? How does he feel about it?"

"I'm sure," Roberta said. "And I'm sure he wants to. When I told him we should get married . . ."

"Roberta," her mother looked shocked.

"Different times, Mother," Roberta answered. "When I

told him, you know what he said?" She looked directly at me and smiled. "He said, 'We can't afford it yet.' That's when I knew."

Her mother understood perfectly. "Don't push him too fast," she said. "Let Nature do what it has to do."

"Mazeltov," I said, looking at the joyful Roberta, at the strong Warshafsky, so perfectly matched, so in love. I turned to Mrs. Baron. "Does it have to be a son?"

Julia Baron looked at Warshafsky appraisingly. He returned her look a bit defiantly, a bit fearfully, it seemed to me, yet with strength and confidence. "No," Julia Baron said to me, quietly. "No, it doesn't."